HONEYMOON SUMMER

HONEYMOON SUMMER

by

Martha Sears West

CLEAN KIND WORLD
Los Angeles

CLEAN KIND WORLD
Los Angeles

Text and Illustrations Copyright © 2020, 2019 by Martha Sears West.
Edited by Page Mallett

Honeymoon Summer
Fourth in Hetty Series

Young Adult/Bildungsroman: This novel is a work of fiction. Names, characters, places, and incidents are either products of the author's imagination or are used fictitiously. All characters are fictional, and any similarity to people living or dead, events, or locales is purely coincidental.

Library of Congress Cataloging-in-Publication Data

Names: West, Martha Sears, 1938- author, illustrator.
Title: Honeymoon summer / by Martha Sears West.
Description: Los Angeles : Probitas Press Clean Kind World Books, [2019] |
    Series: Fourth in Hetty series
Identifiers: LCCN 2019014294 (print) | LCCN 2019015510 (ebook) |
ISBN 978-0-9908693-6-8 (ebook) | ISBN 978-1-7329799-0-1(print)
Subjects: | GSAFD: Love stories.
Classification: LCC PS3623.E8449 (ebook) | LCC PS3623.E8449 H66 2019
(print)
    | DDC 813/.6--dc23
LC record available at https://lccn.loc.gov/2019014294

ISBN 978-1-7329799-1-8 (audio)

Honeymoon Summer takes place in the Summer of 1960,
after the conclusion of *Hetty or Not*

CleanKindWorldBooks.com   ParkPlacePress.com
Toll Free 800·616·8081 · Fax 323·953·9850 · Shipping 435·764·4545
2016 Cummings · Los Angeles CA 90027
ymaddox@CleanKindWorldBooks.com

Martha Sears West titles are available online and in fine bookstores:
· *Jake, Dad and the Worm* · *Longer Than Forevermore* ·
· *Rhymes and Doodles from a Wind-up Toy* ·

· *Hetty* · *Hetty Happens* · *Hetty or Not* · *Honeymoon Summer* · *Hetty on Hold* ·
are available in print, audio, and eBook.

10 9 8 6 5 4 3 2 1
Printed in the United States of America

Marriage is a fine and sacred thing if you make it so.
—*William Lyon Phelps*

CONTENTS

ILLUSTRATIONS

CHARACTERS

Hetty Morganthal, *age 20*

Morgan Morganthal, *age 24*

Ben, né Heinrich O'Malley Benutto, *elderly traveler*

Sophie, *Ben's traveling companion*

Stewie, *age 12, son of Sophie*

Troy Sofer, *artist*

Miko Kawada, *age 19*

Mr. Kawada, *father of Miko*

Katrinka Wallace, *age 27, Morgan's former fiancée*

CHAPTER ONE

Athlete's Foot

The plane shuddered, and Morgan reassured Hetty with a firm hand.

"On your honeymoon?" asked the stewardess. She was passing out gum and cigarettes. Hetty blushed. Was her nervous giddiness so apparent?

Morgan answered for them both. "Yes, my wife and I leave for Europe tomorrow."

At the word *wife,* Hetty felt a great swelling of joy and wanted to burst into song. *Rule, Brittania!* came to mind—with a full orchestra and a crowd of thousands waving flags and shouting, "Hetty loves Morgan Morganthal!"

The stewardess raised a painted eyebrow and spoke with particular attention to Morgan. "It's good we can fly nowadays." She moved closer to his ear, as if to share an intimate secret. "I would *never* go by ship."

"Actually," Hetty said, "we'll be going by ocean liner. The *Queen Mary.*"

The stewardess formed her mouth into a little rosebud. "Really? I had a friend on the *Andrea Doria* when she sank. But that was 1956, and nothing like it has happened in the four years since then." She smiled sweetly at Morgan and walked away.

People were drawn to Morgan, but Hetty felt no resentment. As always, he handled the attention with tact.

"Morgan, how could she tell we're on our honeymoon?"

"By my foolish expression?"

"But you look normal."

"Well," he whispered, "I'm not. I feel like a man possessed." The corners of his eyes crinkled with the beginnings of a smile.

Hetty closed her eyes. "Is there some other way to say that?"

"Oh, I just mean I'm glad we belong to each other . . . at last."

She blinked. "That's better."

In the aisle, the stewardess oozed grace and confidence. Her hair was smoothed into an elegant French roll and tucked neatly under her jaunty cap. Hetty felt tall and shapeless. She slumped down in her seat, hoping to look shorter than Morgan. But no amount of wishing would ever tame the pale, unruly hair that floated around her face. She had long ago despaired of managing it.

"Morgan," she said, "I need you to . . . to hold my hand."

He did, but his eyes were serious and his lips firm. Slowly, he turned Hetty's wedding band around and around on her finger as if something was on his mind. Perhaps he was thinking of the Ferris wheel he and his father wanted to purchase. Two weeks from now, he would have to leave her briefly and go to Germany. Or was it Czechoslovakia? As legal counsel for the Morganthal Circus, he would enter negotiations with the manufacturer.

A vivid memory came to Hetty. She had been twelve at the time. Her best friend Melinda Morganthal took her to watch a dazzling circus performance. They sat on the front row near the center ring. In the spotlights, a magnificent figure wearing a mask and a flowing cape entered on a white horse.

Even after he dismounted and stood before them, Melinda didn't mention it was her older brother, Morgan. Throwing back his cape, he raised a silver thimble in his white-gloved hand. The corner of a gossamer scarf peeked out from it. At first, he pulled at the little corner, easing it out ever so gently. Then faster and faster, until suddenly it engulfed the space with a wondrous explosion of silk.

Hetty's thoughts returned to the present when the plane rocked. Morgan pressed her hand, as if he could sense her unease. Could he feel her blissful elation as well? If so, maybe he would approach it slowly at first, out of respect for her private thoughts. Then at his touch, her boundless joy would billow beyond control, posing a safety hazard for the other passengers.

She pictured floating with him on a cloud of white silk. He would lift her higher and higher to the heavens . . . to a place clear and bright in the pure brilliance of the sun.

Morgan shifted restlessly. He appeared to be composing his thoughts. A dark thatch of hair fell over his forehead, and he pressed her hand to his lips. There was such kindness and love in the depth of his eyes, she could hardly breathe. Hetty lowered her gaze to control the intensity of her feelings.

"What is it, Morgan?" She put her head on his shoulder. In silence, he continued to turn the ring.

When he spoke, it was almost to himself. "Where should I start . . ."

His hand required an answer, so she clasped it tightly and said, "Anywhere. Just anywhere at all."

"I want to be a good husband, Hetty. But I have no idea how to go about it."

She averted her eyes, hoping to make it easier for him. "Of course," she said, "because that's one thing you've never been before." She focused on his knee—the place where the crease in his trousers flattened out. "It's the same with me."

He looked out the window. "I know. But at least you grew up seeing your parents together. I wish I had that. It's just . . . well, there must be rules for husbands."

"Maybe so. I wouldn't know what they are either."

Again, she thought of the crease in his pants. After the honeymoon, it would be her responsibility to put it there. They had received an iron, but she would need an ironing board.

The silence that followed was as puzzling as it was awkward, and Morgan spoke without looking at her. "There are things every couple should discuss before they marry."

The heat crept across Hetty's cheeks until she knew her face must be quite pink. "We sort of did, didn't we? I mean we decided maybe just being in love would . . . you know, make everything happen naturally?"

"But I don't even know things like, well . . . should I shave in the middle of the night?"

"Why would you do that?"

He winced. "My overactive five o'clock shadow."

This seemed to be a genuine concern of his, so Hetty concealed her amusement.

She thought of confiding a concern of her own, but it seemed too silly and personal. It was about things like brushing her teeth—the way she drooled toothpaste so the foam ran down her elbow. If Morgan should see, he'd be disillusioned, for sure!

Hetty had heard of people getting married on board ship. She mused about whether all ships' captains could both perform and annul marriages. Morgan would know, because lawyers always knew things like that.

"I guess we'll have to figure things out together," she said.

Morgan's expression was somber. "My summer job with the Forest Service—that was, uh . . . hardly a lesson in honeymoon etiquette," he said. "And the guys I roomed with in college . . . well, you know."

"So, pretend I'm just another roommate," she said.

"My imagination's good. But not *that* good."

"Then maybe we could do what seems best and vote on what we think works?"

"Ah, yes . . . secret ballots. Heads on our desks." He laughed and lowered his voice. "But what if I got something like . . . oh, say . . . *athlete's foot*?"

Those last two words came out brightly. Morgan's face colored with his obvious failure to make them sound unrehearsed.

So that was it. Somehow, Hetty was comforted to learn his concerns were similar to hers.

"Not too romantic," he said mournfully.

"Oh, but it would be, to me!" Hetty said. "Just think how long I've pictured our lives together. All those years we spent apart . . . they felt like forever. I wanted to know *everything* about you. Now I want to watch you cut your toenails and hear you sing in the shower. And . . . you used the word *possessed*. We belong to each other now. So that means your feet are my feet, and mine are yours."

She laughed at her own runaway words. "Anyway, you're athletic and you have feet, so it's only natural." Her ankle was touching Morgan's. She kept it there because she could. After all, his ankle was her ankle now.

The beautiful stewardess returned to serve shrimp cocktail across the aisle. Hetty smiled and positioned her tray in preparation for dinner. Most airlines touted the training centers for their flight attendants as schools for brides. Hetty sincerely hoped for her happiness. Yet no stewardess could possibly experience such happiness as hers. She was sure of it.

But what was that on the floor? "Look, Morgan! It must have been in your cuffs." The guests had thrown handfuls of rice at them after the reception. Now it littered the aisle, publicly proclaiming their recent wedding.

Rice, Hetty thought. *The symbol of fertility. A way of wishing us lots of babies. Our friends meant well, but they didn't know what the doctor told us.*

He said I mustn't have children. Not ever.

Something Less Sturdy

It was late when the plane landed in New York. Hours had passed since Hetty had two tall glasses of lemonade on the plane. She was eager to find a ladies' room but hesitated to say so. Morgan hailed a taxi to take them directly to the Plaza Hotel. Hetty was surprised. How could they afford to stay in such an expensive place?

When they arrived, a bellman hurried toward them. "Mr. Morganthal, sir!"

In the dark, all Hetty could see of his face was a broad, animated grin. But Morgan knew him right away and said, "Good to see you, Jim. How's the family?"

She could guess what Jim would do after work: he would gather his family around him and announce that on this very day of May, in the year 1960, Morgan Morganthal actually called him by name! With a reverent hush, they would open a scrapbook and review newspaper articles they had collected about him.

Readers mistakenly assumed the handsome Morgan would inherit the vast Morganthal business empire—a conglomerate reaching beyond the world of insurance, shipbuilding, and cosmetics. All this was meant to happen upon his fairy-tale marriage to Katrinka Wallace.

His skills in the Morganthal Circus were enough to keep him in the public eye. In addition, there would be headings like: *Stock Surges as Morgan Rises in Morganthal Business Empire; Morganthal Refuses to Run for Congress; Heartthrob Morganthal Dumps Beauty Queen to Wed Brainy Unknown.*

Jim led them up the elevator and along the plush carpeting of the corridors, exchanging friendly small talk. On the fourth floor, he stopped before a wide door and turned a brass key in the lock. The next few minutes were a blur of suitcases and luggage racks. Morgan shook Jim's hand and thanked him with a tip.

Hetty marveled at Morgan's easy confidence in every situation and with all people. How could the two of them be more different?

The spacious room glowed in the warmth of the satin bedding and crystal chandeliers. Morgan said, "Our home for the night," and the door snapped shut.

As long as she could recall, Hetty had wanted to belong to Morgan. She thought of the many letters of longing during their self-imposed separation. Not even the years of imagining their lives together prepared Hetty for the fullness of her joy.

But, also on her mind was the fullness of her bladder.

The city lights flashed through the window. Morgan kissed her forehead and smoothed back her hair. "What would you like to do?"

"Well, um . . . maybe . . . I guess I might brush my teeth."

He helped her off with her jacket and hung it on a thick wooden hanger.

She immediately regretted mentioning her teeth. Shutting the bathroom door would look silly now, as if such a thing required privacy. If she had spoken frankly of feeling awkward, they could have laughed about it. At some point, this would all become easy.

An idea came to her. "Maybe I could organize my suitcase while you go in there. If you, I mean . . . I think if you use the sink first, and shower and everything."

He glanced at his watch. "Yes, maybe it's that time."

She could run down to the restroom in the lobby while he was in the bathroom. That could work if she hurried. The minute Hetty heard Morgan turn on the shower, she took the elevator down.

Oh, dear! Where was the ladies' room? Wasn't it just left of the restaurant? She tried to appear at ease, as if looking around for the fun of it. But that was impossible, with the urgency she felt.

Ah! There it was, just in time.

At the wash basin, Hetty saw her disheveled appearance in the mirror. *Can such a person fit into Morgan's life?* She had thrived in a simple and happy home, with wise and loving parents—something Morgan said he always missed in his life.

Hetty thought of the Morganthals' opulent lifestyle. Earlier in their marriage, Max and Mimi Morganthal considered alcohol and lavish parties more important than their children. Even at the age of seven, Morgan took a surprising amount of responsibility for his three-year-old sister. Then as a teenager, he attended her school PTA meetings.

Suddenly, Hetty's breathing became rapid and shallow. *Our room! Where is it? What floor?* Biting her lip, she straightened her spine.

Starting with the fifth floor, she searched. *The doors all look the same. The room number must be on the key.* Her face flushed with distress. The key was in her purse in the room! The heat spread from her temples into her scalp.

After considering the options, she tapped timidly on what she hoped would be the right door. It opened as far as the chain allowed—enough to reveal an irritated man she had roused from a sound sleep.

"Oh, I'm sorry . . ." Before she finished her apology, he slammed the door.

I mustn't keep getting lost—it seems so immature. Jim gave us two keys. Maybe that's all there were.

After a frantic search for Jim, she found him on the sixth floor.

"Jim! I'm so glad to see you . . . I don't have my key."

He bowed a little and gave her a kindly smile. "Yes ma'am, Mrs. Morganthal! I reckon you got yourself the wrong floor.

That'll never do, us losin' Mr. Morganthal's new missus! No, ma'am! Just you follow me."

Morgan must have heard them talking. He opened the door, wearing blue and white striped pajamas and acting as if everything was normal. There was no mention of her disappearance, and Hetty was grateful for his sensitivity. She feared thanking him might undo the effect of it.

Apparently, he had cut himself shaving. A small piece of toilet paper was stuck to his neck. Hetty was sure he left it there purposely to usher in a new informality, and she loved him for it. She wanted to feel his smooth cheeks, but she wasn't sure what should come next.

Morgan flashed a smile and indicated the door to the bathroom. "It's all yours. I left a few things in there. I hope you don't mind." His smooth leather case nestled in the corner of the marble counter.

Hetty fingered a narrow silver tray, admiring the small crystal bottles and jars on it. A frilly shower cap with the hotel logo proved large enough to contain her hair. And in the shower, there were three gold-plated shower heads. None of them required the constant adjusting Hetty was accustomed to.

The only place she had seen such elegance was in Morgan's home. The Morganthals had a large tapestry gallery with a gold-stenciled ceiling, an indoor gymnasium, and a music room with deep red damask walls and two grand pianos.

The soothing shower did nothing to keep Hetty's mind from racing. She had a lot of thinking to do, and it was all so complicated.

She thought of the night before Morgan was supposed to marry Katrinka.

Morgan didn't know my heart was broken. He came to tell me goodbye. When I couldn't contain my misery, he confessed to having the same feelings. Suddenly everything was turned upside down. It was clear he couldn't go through with the wedding.

Calling it off meant Morgan would forfeit his inheritance. But losing his father's approval was even harder for him.

Everything about Morgan is fine and good. When I think of all he sacrificed to marry me, how can I possibly live up to his expectations?

After quickly drying herself, Hetty tightened the towel around her thin form. She decided against unfolding the white chenille robe the hotel provided—or opening the bottle of rosewater. If she did, the hotel might charge extra. Her family had known how to be frugal. Now that Morgan wouldn't inherit the Morganthal wealth, would he learn to be careful with money?

She opened her well-worn overnight case with its scuffed corners. The one she used for doll clothes just ten years back. Folded on top was the soft new nightgown her mother had made. It matched the blue of her eyes. But best of all, the neckline hid most of the scar from her heart operation.

Eventually Hetty would have to leave the bathroom. Maybe she wouldn't look so bony if she could hide behind her hair. But while brushing out the wayward tangles, she reconsidered and gathered her billowing curls in a blue satin ribbon.

The future I've dreamed of is now. Am I ready? With a glance in the mirror, she straightened her spine. *Hetty, set, go!*

She opened the door a few timid inches. Morgan was sitting at the foot of the bed waiting for her. He stood as she entered, and his hand reached for her. "May I have this dance?" The deep blue of his eyes reflected the warmth of her own intense happiness.

She felt herself melting at the touch of his hand and the fresh scent of his skin. He was the only partner Hetty had ever wanted. When dancing with others, she had to imagine they were Morgan. Her cheeks flushed with dreams and memories yet to be made.

"Or we could just stand like this," he said, "and hope for some music."

She put her cheek against his. "That could be a very long time."

"That's the whole idea."

"Or," she whispered, "you could sing."

"No, I couldn't."

"Your sister says you used to sing her to sleep."

His other arm tightened around her waist. "She was pretending to fall asleep, so I'd stop."

"I don't care what you sing, I won't pretend to fall asleep."

"I don't know . . ." He was quiet for a time. It was enough that he was holding her. But when the dancing began, he provided the music.

"Found a peanut, found a peanut . . ." He guided her slowly around the room.

Hetty's voice joined his. "Ate it anyway, ate it anyway . . ." They swayed to their own duet. All past memories were becoming a blur. Home was here now, with Morgan.

"My feet keep catching in my nightgown."

"Somehow, I expected you to be a pajama person."

"Actually, I am. But Mother thought you'd like to see me in something less . . . um . . . sturdy."

"It depends. For instance, you'd need pajamas, to jump on the bed."

"But that was never allowed."

"We can make our own rules," he said.

Hetty thought a kiss would be nice about now, and Morgan did not disappoint her. Soon they resumed their dancing. His strength and agility evoked in her an exhilarating grace and they moved as one. This pleasurable unity led her to the vision she had long held of their future:

I hope we can work and think together in all aspects of our marriage . . . in all our most important decisions.

Morgan knows I applied to law school. I want him to be happy about it, but he might not like the idea. How should I tell him I've been accepted?

Maybe I'll think of a way tomorrow.

Over the Moon

Morgan knew next to nothing about nightgowns and was overwhelmed by the feminine blue softness he held gathered in his arms. He soon learned such gowns were not designed for dancing. His vague but joyous bewilderment may have contributed to the accident that occurred.

Hetty stepped on the hem of her nightgown, and Morgan's legs became entangled in its folds. Helpless to soften her fall, he felt responsible when her head bumped against the nightstand. He offered profuse apologies—and consolation of the sort he was eager to provide. Some things take time, and he was never one to do things halfway.

Morgan had entered his marriage with a keen sense of responsibility.

When he was sixteen, his sister brought Hetty to their home to play jump-rope. The girls were twelve at the time, and it was a friendship he encouraged his sister to cultivate. His instinct was to watch over them both.

When Hetty was seventeen, a sudden change in Morgan's feelings came almost without warning. He was rather puzzled by the increased intensity of his desire to care for her.

Even now this was a delicious facet of their relationship.

For years, he had struggled to conquer the quickening of his pulse in her presence. The fervor of his feelings had been among the reasons for their decision to stay apart, but the nightmare of their four-year separation was now over.

Hetty's cheeks flushed under his gaze, and the lights formed a halo in the softness of her hair. Her eyes, soft with wonder, spoke of her purity. How could he live to deserve the love and trust shining in her countenance?

Unaccustomed as they were to the intimacy of marriage, Morgan had long assumed Hetty would need a period of adjustment. Those concerns proved to be unfounded. She received him with a warmth beyond his wildest expectations.

Before he knew it, the morning sun shimmered through the silken draperies. Hetty remained asleep, and he listened for a time to her quiet breathing. The slightest smile turned up one corner of her mouth. Her eyes moved rapidly, and he knew her dream was of him. Her lips opened slightly. They were soft and pink, and he imagined tasting them again.

Her hair tumbled over the side of the bed. The ribbon that held it in place got lost in the night and was now stuck to her cheek.

From this time forward, the world might seem unchanged to others. Planets would continue in their orbit; he and Hetty would board the *Queen Mary* today and sail on schedule. There would be lunches and dinners; talking to friends and strangers; putting on socks and shoes.

But Morgan knew nothing would ever be the same again, and he was deeply satisfied.

Toast and Tears

Was someone knocking on the door of their room? Hetty kept her eyes tightly closed for her dream to continue.

The door opened to admit the rattle of a teacart. Bacon, pancakes, syrup—and was it buttered toast she smelled?

Morgan's warm breath was on her cheek, and her arms went around his neck. A dark shock of hair hid his eyebrows. "I haven't shaved. Don't let me scratch you."

"I want you to, so I'll know this is real."

Morgan flashed a smile. "Take my word for it."

Her fingers traced the line of his jaw and lingered on his lips. "I want this dream to go on forever."

Amusement crinkled the corners of his eyes. "And miss the ship?"

Hetty sighed with happiness and sat upright. Morgan stuffed a pillow behind her back and laid a white linen napkin across her lap. On the teacart were fresh strawberries and

English muffins in a silver toast rack. This was the perfect first day of the rest their lives. Nothing could dampen so great a joy.

Then she saw them. Three tiny pink rosebuds. They seemed to smirk at her from the slender vase on her tray. Her neck jerked at the sight.

Katrinka chose a bouquet of miniature pink rosebuds for her wedding to Morgan. The wedding that didn't happen, because of me. But I can't think about that. She isn't Morgan's fiancée anymore. We're free of her. At least on our honeymoon.

I'll always remember their wedding cake melting in the sun. The pink roses drooping.

Hetty tried to cover her distress, but her voice was thin and far away. "It's . . . it's too elegant," she said. "I mean isn't it too expensive?" Whatever Morgan had just said, she knew her response was unrelated.

"No, it's fine," he said. "You don't need to worry."

"I don't know . . . I mean, do we really need it . . ." her voice trailed off.

Disappointment showed in Morgan's serious expression.

"I wanted it for you," he said. The joy was gone.

He was trying his best to please her, and she had broken the spell. She had crushed his happiness. Her cheeks were hot with remorse.

Between years of law school, he had worked for the Forest Service. His letters had been full of dreams. In spite of the danger, he fought forest fires to pay for occasions such as this.

Tears filled Hetty's eyes. "I'm so sorry . . . I'm grateful. It's a beautiful breakfast." Her voice quivered. "Thank you. You're so kind." If she could eat it, he would see her appreciation, but the lump in her throat made it impossible.

They had been married only one day, and a confusion of irrational sensations had already seized her. While trying to hide her senseless insecurities, she had been careless with words. Tears, large and profuse, flowed down her cheeks, and without warning, her sobs came in waves. Morgan held her close.

Hetty could give no logical explanation in response to his concerns. But when she could speak again, she suggested maybe her heart was breaking from too much love.

"Is that such a bad way to go?" he asked. "If we just laugh a little, everything will be all right. I promise."

She believed him, but for some unknown reason, even as they laughed together, she struggled to control her tears.

In childhood, before her bedtime, Hetty often listened to a robin singing its evening song. After it stopped, she wished for a way to remember the sound of it all through the night. So, from that time on, she held her breath and listened carefully with her eyes closed. Maybe that was the way to keep a dream alive, too.

"Morgan," she said, "I'm sorry. I didn't mean to . . . I offended you."

He kissed away a tear. "You couldn't possibly offend me. I love you too much."

CHAPTER TWO

Table for Eight

Hetty and Morgan followed the other passengers down the broad staircase to the dining room.

This would be their first lunch on the *Queen Mary*. The immense mural on the landing was visible from all corners of the expansive room. Everywhere, fresh flowers harmonized with the luxurious furnishings. Many of the tables were already occupied by passengers in festive attire—some laughing, others looking at their menus.

At each place setting, the silverware spread far enough in both directions to alarm Hetty. She never had to contend with so many courses. Whatever Morgan did, she would have to watch and do the same.

"There's space at that table," Morgan said. "It only has two people."

Hetty followed his eyes. "Yes, they look nice. I hope they speak English."

When they approached, an Asian gentleman stood to greet them warmly. "Please, please," he said, "sit." Bowing several times, he introduced himself as Kawada Tatsuo. "And my daughter, Mariko." He bowed again.

With a shy glance, the girl said, "They call me Miko back home."

Hetty took the seat next to her. "Where's home?"

"I grew up in San Francisco."

Hetty assumed Miko was about fifteen, but soon learned her looks were deceiving. She was a student at Stanford University.

Soon three more people joined them. A man of about seventy limped in their direction, and two others followed. The first of these was a nervous woman, probably in her forties, wearing an orchid. She introduced herself as Sophie. Her sullen twelve-year-old son said his name was Stewie.

Taking the chair next to Morgan, the man hung his cane on the back of it. "Heinrich O'Malley Benutto's the name," he said. "Just call me Ben. And no, I can't imagine what my parents were thinking!" When he laughed and slapped his knees, his horn-rimmed glasses slipped down his nose. Sophie appeared to recognize that as her cue to laugh with him.

Morgan greeted Sophie and Stewie. In the process of making introductions all around, he called the Japanese gentleman Mr. Tatsuo.

He received another bow and a cheerful request. "Please . . . it's Kawada."

Miko explained on behalf of her father. "It's the Japanese way. We say the family name first." Her father nodded.

"So . . ." Hetty said, "that means they call you Kawada-san?"

He smiled agreeably. "Hai! Yes, yes."

Sophie fidgeted with her place setting while her son continued to sulk. Hetty wondered if being twelve was the cause of his ill humor, or if it was the boy's default expression. And did Ben have some degree of control over them both?

Hetty was concerned about the unoccupied seat next to Stewie, and a solution was slow in coming. But at last a gentleman placed his hand on the back of it. "I'm Troy Sofer," he said. "May I?" As a courtesy, the question was directed at Stewie.

Before sitting next to Stewie, Troy shook his hand and aimed a cheerful salute toward the others. Almost from the start, he and Stewie were deep in conversation.

Hetty recalled seeing Troy before. Was it during the boarding process? Yes, she'd seen him this morning behind Morgan, waiting to show his passport. His hair was slightly gray at the temples, but a more distinguishing feature was his rather elegant long nose. His eyes darted everywhere, suggesting a keen mind and lively interest in his surroundings.

Before long they all experienced the easy familiarity of old friends. Attention often centered on Morgan, but he was skilled at redirecting the spotlight.

Hetty inclined her head toward Miko. "What's your final destination?"

"Father and I are going to Japan. I'm supposed to get married in Tokyo."

"Oh, you must be excited!" said Hetty. "Tell me about your fiancé."

"I haven't met him yet." Miko locked eyes with Hetty, as if she had more to tell.

Whatever Troy was saying elicited the word *cool* from Stewie many times over. Hetty was delighted to see the boy was no longer brooding. The change in Stewie also affected his mother's expression. Sophie gave Troy an appreciative smile that melted years from her face.

The eight new acquaintances were so congenial that they didn't let the buttered lobster tails interfere with their conversation. More than once, the waiter removed a course untouched.

After the meal was over, the group seemed likely to linger in the dining room. Morgan hinted at the lateness of the hour and stood as a signal to the others. From his position behind Hetty's seat, he placed one hand on her shoulder. Hetty's heartbeat became rapid, and she turned all soft inside.

Suddenly she was desperate to feel his other hand. It was a fierce, irrational desperation. Surely, everyone within view could sense she was unable to breathe or swallow normally.

Now he was pulling out her chair. *Please Morgan . . . oh, please touch me again. If you don't, I think I'll die of love, right here on the floor of the* Queen Mary.

The vibrations of his voice reached her deep inside, melting into the softness. How long must she wait, pretending to hear like everyone else? She imagined they were floating together like eagles, with his wings enfolding her. She felt herself hovering nearby while he spoke of ordinary things.

But he was still talking to the others. "Such good company is a pleasure," he said. "We should spend more time this way."

Troy leapt to his feet and made a proposal in a loud voice. "I say let's *make* it happen!" There was a general hum of agreement, so it was decided they would meet again.

Morgan pulled out Hetty's chair. His hands were only two inches from the place her shoulder had been.

Touch me now, Morgan! I can endure the waiting, if you do. Or I'll waste away from love. When they lay me on the floor, I'll need you to lie down next to me. I'll love you just the same, even if I'm dead.

You could cover me with the white linen cloth from our table. The waiter removed the crumbs between courses, so it's mostly clean. That place where Stewie spilled cherry sauce could go over my feet. Please have them vacuum carefully around me so I won't get sucked up in the vacuum cleaner.

And please don't cover me with miniature pink rosebuds.

They mounted the curved staircase to exit the dining room. Hetty turned to look back at the place where she had nearly expired from the intensity of love. Morgan put his arm around her. Was there a special significance to it?

Yes . . . maybe he had a close call, too.

Something Like That

Hetty pulled a green knit dress over her head and tied the sash. They might walk around the promenade deck and feel the sea breeze. The clothes she wore at lunch wouldn't be warm enough.

She stood behind Morgan, where the mirror reflected them both. She slid her arms around his chest, hoping he liked them there. He winked at her image and felt for the buttons of his flannel shirt.

Before their marriage, Hetty never allowed herself to see Morgan as others did. For years she had loved him for his kindness—a gentle goodness that made her want to try harder; to rise higher; to do anything to deserve his friendship.

Now everything about him filled her with wonder. She was free to admire his strong jaw and earnest blue eyes—his superior mind and body. She was almost startled by his finely chiseled features. To Morgan such attributes, including family wealth, seemed irrelevant, except as connected to a worthy character.

While he fumbled with his cuffs, Hetty reluctantly moved her arms away. She hoped he would draw her hands tight around him again after finishing with the buttons.

Instead, Morgan turned and pulled her close. His hands trembled at her waist. "You make me crazy, Hetty. I can't even button my shirt."

They laughed with a shared awareness. Eventually they would have to leave their stateroom. Daily life must continue—Breakfast. Lunch. Dinner. Sitting close to Morgan at the table. How could she endure such unbearable joy? They would be forced to suffer the sweet agony of anticipation through every course.

"Morgan, is love the same for other people?"

"No." His breath on her neck was warm and exquisite. She thrilled at his kiss. Delirious with joy, she felt herself drowning in their moment of pleasure.

Was that a knock at the door? They froze in place. With luck, whoever it was might give up and go away.

But the next knock was more persistent.

Morgan opened the door. "Stewie!"

"Hi . . . um, what're you guys doing?"

Morgan grinned. "Answering the door."

Stewie shuffled his feet. "Yeah, well . . ." He entered and flopped onto the hassock.

Morgan and Hetty sat together on the bed facing him.

Unlike the sullen boy they saw earlier, Stewie's wide-eyed face was lively and amiable.

"I'm not married," he said, "but I figure seeing as how you—I mean I don't know about stuff like—whatever." He gulped the air with excitement. "Anyhow, my mom's real cool. My friends—their moms are, you know . . ." Stewie rolled his eyes. Perhaps to demonstrate how goofy some mothers seemed compared to his. "We just got *us*, you know, and that's great. At least it *was*. But now with Ben . . ." He sighed. "Ben wants to get rid of me at this boarding school. Can he do stuff like that? I mean, everything's real messed up."

Morgan nodded, and Hetty cocked her head as an aid to comprehension.

Stewie was not ready to rest his case. "How am I supposed to be, you know, man of the house, if he sends me away? I can't take care of her if I'm gone. Ben thinks I'm. . . you know." Morgan appeared to know, but Hetty did not. The way Stewie's tongue lolled out—was that a secret guy-thing?

She meant to listen, but the gentle rocking motion of the ship moved Morgan's arm against hers. She felt his muscles through the fabric of his shirt, and he smelled like a fresh mountain breeze. She imagined standing with him on a mountain peak, leaning into the wind, when suddenly his hands would encircle her waist, lifting her high above the clouds. The thrill left her panting breathlessly. An ocean of words, swirling and dancing, gathered to Morgan. Through open sky, past moon and stars, he drew them in.

Stewie's deep sigh jolted Hetty back to the present. He chewed on his thumbnail and glared out the porthole. "But I'm *not* a dunce."

He did that thing with his tongue again. This time Hetty understood. "Anyhow, Ben made my mom cry. He says she'll always be an old maid. So, what's wrong with that? I mean, if she wants, she can be a real terrific old maid. So, here's my idea: I'll pretend to be Troy and Mom can pretend to be herself. We'll practice how she bumps into Troy accidentally on purpose. Not dumb like in the cartoons. You know—more friendly. She could say, *Oh, hello, Mr. Sofer!* Then maybe he'll say, *You can call me Troy!* or something romantic like that."

Stewie's eyes lit up with another equally inspired idea. "Then next time she can say, *It's nice weather we're having, Troy.*" Looking from Morgan to Hetty, he asked, "So you and her — is that how *you* did it? I mean, to start out?"

Morgan leaned forward. "Something like that."

"Neat! That's what I thought, 'cause you're not all stupid and lovey-dovey, if you know what I mean."

That was accepted as a compliment.

Stewie stood tall as possible and raised his chest. He and Morgan now had a bond—something big in common. They were both experts in matters of the heart.

International Relations

The steward set another place at the dinner table.

"We're honored, Captain Bonnard," Morgan said. "Thank you for joining us."

The captain grinned at the faces around the table. "I know where the fun is." He stroked his beard. "I ought to, by now. I'm about to retire."

Soon a heaping entrée of bouillabaisse was set before the captain. Unfazed by the fishy odor, Captain Bonnard tackled it with the gusto of a caveman. His spoon circled the air above the steaming stew like a shark circling its prey.

Hetty was glad she hadn't ordered anything so frightening. Her braised sweetbread dish was delicious. However, she did not wish to hear of its anatomical function or to which animal it once belonged.

"I sought out the Morganthals here," the captain said. "You know how it is. In my line of work, you know who's who in the shipbuilding business."

Ben glanced at Morgan. Then jerking his head back, he averted his eyes.

The captain leaned forward on his elbows and slurped on a clamshell. "I want to hear about the rest of you," he said.

The first to speak was Troy. "This is a magnificent ship. And age has not diminished her beauty." He glanced at Sophie. She seemed to notice and blushed. "What I mean is . . I admire the art deco—especially the Charles Pears and Duncan Carse paintings."

Captain Bonnard nodded. "You should have seen *The Queen Mary* in her glory days." His fingers rummaged around and retrieved a black mussel shell. "I'm afraid competition with the airlines is hurting the ocean liners. People are in too big a hurry to get places these days."

Troy shook his head. "It's a real shame."

"That's an artist talking," explained Morgan. "Troy's been pointing out some details we might not have noticed."

The captain licked his fingers and glanced at Troy. "So, you're an artist. What takes you abroad?"

"My brother. L. B. and I did everything together growing up. Same schools and college. We both studied in France. When I went back to the States, L. B. stayed in Paris to build his career. He's an artist too. The cadmium and lead in paints have ruined his health. I'd like to take him home with me. He says he's okay, but I've got to see for myself."

The captain pointed a fork at Stewie. "And what about you, young man?" He burped and excused himself cheerily.

Stewie appeared stymied by the general question, so Hetty helped out. "He's turning thirteen this month," she said.

"So, Grandpa brought you and Mom along to celebrate?"

Ben corrected him. "I'm *not* his grandpa." He cleared his throat for punctuation. "I hired Sophie when I needed a housekeeper. Stewie just came with the package."

As if hoping for a change of subject, Stewie scowled. But Ben continued. "At first it was supposed to be a short-term arrangement, just while I've got this bad leg."

Hetty noticed something odd. Sophie looked to Ben as if she needed permission to speak. He didn't give it, and Hetty wondered why.

The captain moved on with another question. "Let's see now . . . Mr. Kawada, is it?" With a good-humored laugh, he slapped Mr. Kawada on the back. "No hard feelings, right? About the war, I mean."

This gesture of fellowship appeared to puzzle Mr. Kawada. After an unsettling interval, he returned the courtesy with an indecisive thump on the captain's back. Though Captain Bonnard had seemed ready to resume eating, he delayed briefly to allow for this pleasant international exchange.

"I know you've got to be brilliant to speak Japanese," he said. "I mean, don't you have all kinds of alphabets?" He laughed and twirled his mustache. "Even children in Japan know when to say *domo* or *dozo*. But I can't remember which is which, unless I write them on an index card." He raised his bushy eyebrows. "I speak a little Japanese—*sukoshi*, that is. *Sayonara* means goodbye, right?"

"Hai . . . yes, yes!" Mr. Kawada's head bobbed up and down. "Captain is real Japanese!"

"Thank you." Captain Bonnard beamed modestly at the approval. "That's about all I know. But enough about me. You come from the states. Were you there long?"

"Ah, yes. Miko is born California, before War. We move back to San Francisco in 1945."

"Where were you during the War?"

"Wartime Relocation Camp, three and a half year. In Topaz."

"Really? Nasty business. I know Topaz. It was in Utah. My mother grew up near there." He shook his head. "Bad, bad business!"

"Hai! But . . . not bad anymore. All Topaz set free Halloween day, 1945."

"Halloween? You don't say! What'll you do now?"

"We go home to Japan. Father-in-law die last year and have no one to head family business—culture pearl business. Only me."

"Yes, yes!" said Captain Bonnard. He held his nose and did his impression of a pearl diver. The two men took turns laughing and diving.

Mr. Kawada thumped the captain on the back. "See? All very good now. No hard feelings."

Even Stewie smiled.

Hetty reflected on the differences in body language across cultures. The rules for bowing and handshaking were complicated enough, and she was sure Mr. Kawada had never been a back-slapper until now. She decided a smile must be the gesture most easily mastered and understood.

Soon dessert interrupted the diving pantomime.

After Dinner

While the dessert dishes were being removed, Captain Bonnard offered a tour of the ship to his new acquaintances at the table. They quickly decided on a time and date for meeting at the bridge. Starting with the engine room, the chief officer would show them around.

Soon the orchestra tuned their instruments. Captain Bonnard said *sayonara*, and the dance music began in earnest. Morgan took Hetty's hand, but Ben held them in conversation before they could slip onto the dance floor. Several dances later, he was still talking. Hetty had to settle for just imagining Morgan's arm around her, guiding her across the floor.

Soon the orchestra launched into the bunny hop, which drew more people from their seats. When Stewie ran to insert himself into the line, Miko followed. Mr. Kawada turned his chair around to watch, with his back erect and his feet firmly planted. Hetty decided he placed himself there as the defender of formality, which was under severe attack.

To record the activity, Troy took out a pencil and sketchbook. He wasn't quite through drawing when the music changed, but he put down his sketchbook and leaned toward Sophie. "You wouldn't care to dance, would you?"

She blinked in surprise. "Thank you, I'm quite happy just watching." She glanced at Ben. "I really don't mind being a spectator."

Ben said, "Don't be silly! Go ahead. If it wasn't for this leg of mine, *I'd* be asking you." He waved them off and turned back to Morgan. "Why bring her on this trip, if she can't have fun? That's the whole point."

While Troy whirled her around the floor, Sophie glanced at Ben several times. When he appeared to bestow permission for her to have fun, her smile was grateful and lively.

Ben laughed. "You think this trip is good enough to grease the wheels? Not a bad orchestra—great dinner. What do you bet she'll marry me before it's over?"

If Ben thought Morgan and Hetty might participate in some prearranged bribe, he was disappointed. His laughter stopped abruptly, and with a gnarled forefinger, he traced an imaginary square on the tablecloth. "I wanted to do something good before I kick the bucket." He looked directly at Morgan. "I'm going to change my will to benefit Sophie. She's making a better man of me. Best housekeeper I ever had." Ben squinted at the dancers. "But I don't know what Sophie sees in that son of hers," he said. He appeared to be in pain. Miko was teaching the foxtrot to Stewie, whose lips were counting, o*ne, two, three, four. One, two, three, four* . . .

Hetty came to Stewie's defense. "He's a good boy. And he seems devoted to his mother."

"I know, I know," said Ben, "a mama's boy with a bad attitude. To be honest, I don't want him around if he can't talk in sentences. I'm sending him away to school in the fall. Phillips Exeter should straighten him out."

Hetty wondered if she should have kept quiet. Maybe it was rude of her to disagree with Ben, but she spoke up again.

"I know Stewie can look cross, but I wonder if he's just hiding his shyness."

Ben shuffled the goblets and wine glasses around in front of him until he found his ginger ale. Ignoring Hetty's words, he addressed Morgan. "My pills don't mix with alcohol," he said. "I notice you don't drink either."

"That's right," Morgan said. "I saw what alcohol did to my parents."

Hetty feared she had embarrassed Morgan by entering the conversation. They all watched the dancers for a time.

After a pause, Ben said, "I've got an obnoxious nephew named Stanley, and he wants to be remembered in my will. He's my only relative. What would *you* do?"

Morgan suppressed a smile. "Your will might say something like, *Hi there, Stanley!* That should do it."

Ben laughed, but his face showed he felt unwell. Excusing himself, he asked Morgan to say good night to Sophie and the others. He leaned heavily on his cane and left for his stateroom.

Morgan was now free to guide Hetty to the dance floor. His nimble grace commanded attention until he swept her out of the spotlights. "I'm glad you're not my housekeeper," he said.

Hetty resolved to be whatever Morgan wanted, as long as she was his.

They spotted Stewie and Miko romping near the center of the floor. Miko appeared completely unaffected by her father's stern posture. Her tousled young partner bounced with vigor from one foot to the other. Perhaps he served as her excuse to abandon decorum.

Ben's surprising approach to courtship was still on Hetty's mind. "Morgan, can you imagine their wedding vows? *Do you, Heinrich Benutto, take this woman to be your lawfully wedded housekeeper?*"

Morgan added, "*. . . to have dinner ready and to hold it in the oven so long as you both shall live?*"

This conversation amused them only briefly. They couldn't help noticing Stewie's obvious pleasure, as he watched his mother dance with Troy.

Feeling rather uneasy about the whole situation, Hetty confessed to having a premonition: Ben's marriage plans were sure to end badly for someone.

Embarrassment

Back in their stateroom for the night, Morgan sat to remove his shoes. "You were quiet at dinner, Hetty. I hope you had a good time."

"I did. It's just that . . . well, sometimes I'm afraid I'll put my foot in my mouth," she said. "But you wouldn't know how that feels."

Amusement brought little crinkles to the corners of his eyes. "Try me," he said. His arms opened, inviting her to his lap.

"I mean it, Morgan. You *always* say the right thing."

"I see. Like when I introduced the Strothers family to the hospital board?"

"I never heard about that," she said.

Hetty loved the way Morgan cradled her. She could have stayed there forever. But the way he held her, did he see her as a child? She decided to stop caring whether he did or not and remained on his lap.

He cleared his throat. "Remember Billy Strothers? He died earlier this year."

"Just by name, but I remember his sons. They were not known for their . . . good judgment."

"Exactly," said Morgan. "In fact, between us, does the word *silly* come to mind?

"Anyway, Billy's widow and his sons appreciated how the hospital cared for him. They wanted to establish an endowment in his name—a huge donation. The press was there . . . the TV cameras. A crowd of hundreds. I invited the family of Billy Strothers to come forward." Morgan took a deep breath. "And I introduced them as *the family of Silly Brothers.*"

Hetty's eyes were wide with surprise and sympathy.

Morgan continued. "Half the room laughed when they realized what I said. Then another wave of people laughed when they caught on. My apology didn't help much."

Hetty struggled to keep from laughing. "You never told me!"

"No. I thought it was best to move on."

So that's the secret to his confidence! He knows how to keep right on going. Hetty knew Morgan tried not to worry about things beyond his control. But if such a thing ever happened to her, she would forever lie awake agonizing about it.

Hetty loved learning from the things he said and did. To thank him, her arms went around his shoulders, and she pressed her cheek against the roughness of his whiskers.

She meant it as an expression of gratitude, but in case she had not made herself clear, she kissed his lips as well. He welcomed the encounter so warmly that Hetty concluded he did not see her as a child. He continued to provide proof of that fact, and she did nothing to discourage him.

More time would surely have passed in this agreeable way, but someone was at the door. Morgan received a telegram which he read quickly. *Western Union* was all Hetty saw before he hid it in the drawer under the Gideon Bible.

"Anything important?"

"No. I'm sorry for the interruption."

Hetty wanted just one more kiss. But would it seem forward to let him know?

Maybe that was not the real issue; Hetty realized she could never get enough of Morgan.

"I'm glad you told me about Billy Strothers," she said. "Somehow, it makes me feel better." She sighed. "The first time I went to your home for dinner, do you know what I said to your mother?"

"What was it?"

"I said, 'Thank you, it was so nice of me to come!'"

Morgan chuckled. "And look where it got you. She couldn't love you more."

As fun as it was to share humiliating experiences, Hetty preferred to leave the rest of hers buried in the past.

But there was one thing more she needed to confess: the elaborate meal service on the ship, or anywhere for that matter, made her feel ill-at-ease. Maybe Morgan could talk her through it.

"Morgan, I couldn't possibly deal with something like bouillabaisse."

"Then don't order it."

"I just mean it as an example. Suppose someone put it in front of me? I'd be worse at it than Captain Bonnard."

"What do you mean?"

"You didn't notice how he ate?"

"I didn't say that."

There was a long silence. Hetty felt petty and childish. Did Morgan mean for her to feel so embarrassed? She had to think about it.

I want to learn from your kindness, Morgan. I reacted like a child, so maybe that's why I feel like one. I should have overlooked the captain's manners the way you did.

She blushed. "That was nice of the captain to arrange a tour of the ship," she said.

"Yes, we'll all enjoy it." He unbuttoned his shirt. "And Hetty . . . you can trust your instincts because you understand people's feelings. Your sensitivity is a rare gift."

He continued. "I know Ben didn't want you to defend Stewie. But I'm glad you had the courage to speak your mind. As for bouillabaisse, I never order it." A smile began with his eyes. "It's too hard to eat with one foot in my mouth."

While Morgan sang in the shower, Hetty pulled up the covers and waited for him. His voice; the gentle creaking of the ship; the smell of the sea air—they all provided the perfect background for the dream she was living. How could love make the world seem so beautiful? She breathed deeply with contentment.

Not even the telegram worried her. If there were a serious problem at home, Morgan would tell her. She could count on him.

On the other hand, maybe he just wanted to protect her from worrying. That was the sort of thoughtful thing he might do.

What if her papa had a heart attack? Maybe Morgan wanted her to get a good night's sleep before telling her the bad news. But wouldn't it be best to face it together? Hetty threw back the covers. She couldn't open the drawer fast enough. Finding the telegram under the Bible, she read it. The blood drained from her face, and she read it again: *Ready to meet you as planned. Kat Wallace.*

Hetty inspected the back of the telegram, then turned it again to the front, wishing it away—hoping she only imagined what it said.

No, it was an ugly reality. And it was not meant for her eyes. After replacing the telegram to its hiding place, she closed the drawer.

I thought we left Katrinka behind. Will you really allow this, Morgan? This summer was meant to be ours alone. Why is she coming?

Hetty got back in bed and pulled the covers up to her chin. She heard Morgan shaving. Turning her face to the wall, she pretended to be asleep.

Before long she felt him get in quietly beside her. The fresh clean smell of him made her heartsick. She wanted to touch his face and thank him for the dream that was now past and gone—the beautiful beginning to their marriage.

Morgan, please explain to me about Katrinka. I'm embarrassed to confess I read the telegram. But if you tell me about it first, I won't have to. Whatever is going on, I'll try to understand. It was inexcusable to pry in your business.

As if to discover whether Hetty was expecting him, Morgan touched her shoulder lightly, with anticipation.

The tears squeezed through Hetty's tightly closed eyes, and she clenched her teeth until he withdrew his hand.

CHAPTER THREE

Into the Storm

The next morning at breakfast, Morgan noticed Hetty wasn't quite herself. He wondered if she might be a little seasick. There was talk was of an approaching hurricane, though Captain Bonnard expected to skirt the worst of it. Meanwhile, those who ventured to the dining room were either completely ignorant of the predicted storm or welcomed the adventure.

Stewie eagerly speculated about the use of lifeboats. According to him, Ben was still in his room, and Sophie was making sure he was comfortable. Stewie was more cheerful and talkative than usual, and Morgan assumed it was because Ben was missing.

Troy asked Morgan what he and Hetty planned on doing after the honeymoon.

Morgan threw his head back and laughed. "The honeymoon will never be over." Then he said, "We'll be living in a cottage Hetty's father once owned—a quiet place next to a forest. The climbing roses always need attention."

"Also," Hetty said, "the governor just appointed Morgan to the state ethics commission. We don't know how involved he'll be."

Troy wanted to hear more. "How did that come about?"

"Well," Morgan said, "there's a new Federal Commission on Ethics. When I told the governor about it, he wanted to form a similar group on the state level. By now, he may have chosen others."

"What's ethics?" Stewie asked.

"To sum it up," Morgan said, "it's how we behave when nobody's watching. Being ethical means doing the right thing—even if you're the only one who knows it."

Stewie blinked. "I don't get it. I mean if nobody's watching, how do you know who's doing *bad* stuff?"

"What do *you* think?"

Stewie thought for a minute. "Um . . . maybe we *don't*. I mean I guess we all gotta figure it out ourselves."

"Exactly," said Morgan. "Even when you have the *legal* right to do something, that doesn't always make it the right thing to do. It's knowing the difference between the two, then acting accordingly."

"But if everybody did like that, they wouldn't need your ethics club."

"True," laughed Morgan, "and that way I could spend more time pruning roses."

Mr. Kawada arrived alone, wearing a cheerful face. When Hetty asked about Miko, he said, "Not come to breakfast. Dutiful daughter in writing room, long, long time."

There was something of more concern to Morgan than the conversation. Why did Hetty seem so distracted? He felt for her hand under the table.

He suddenly thought of something she might enjoy. "After breakfast," he said, "should we all go see the carousel?"

Stewie rolled his eyes to express complete lack of interest. Morgan soon realized a twelve-year-old boy is compelled to look bored with childish things.

"As long as he runs the Morganthal Circus," Hetty said, "Morgan needs to look at anything related to it."

Stewie said, "Okay. For business." Hetty had provided the necessary excuse.

As the ship lurched, a general murmur arose from the passengers.

Soon Sophie was seen stumbling toward the table. Stewie pulled the chair out for her, the way he had seen Morgan do it for Hetty. When his mother was seated, he whispered to Troy, "Did I do it right?" His manly pride was obvious.

"Yes, you were extremely suave."

Sophie ordered milk toast for Ben, and Stewie declared, "That's old people food."

Another mighty wave pounded the ship. "Well," said Hetty, "something digestible like that makes sense, with the storm coming."

"Hey," said Stewie, "maybe he'll die from throwing up or something."

"That's not the kind of thing people die of," said Troy.

Stewie shrugged. "I know, but I wouldn't care if he did."

"Ben used to be the same age as you," said Hetty. "You might like him more if you think of it that way."

"Oh." That idea seemed new to Stewie. He looked to Morgan, then back at Hetty.

Sophie put a pat of butter on the floating toast. When standing with it, she seemed rather unsteady. Troy offered to carry it for her. The ship shuddered with another attack from the sea as they left together.

"Cool!" said Stewie.

Hetty wanted to include everyone in their visit to the carousel. Turning to Mr. Kawada, she asked, "So, Miko's not coming?"

"Hai! Yes."

"Wonderful. We'll wait for her."

He laughed and clapped his hands together. "You ask if Miko is not coming. I answer yes, she is not. So sorry . . . in English, *yes* means very different thing!" He bowed. "Today, dutiful daughter is compose very big, long letter in writing room. Yes, and taking very much time. I think daughter say *sayonara* to American boyfriend now." He appeared ready to celebrate.

Stewie grinned at Hetty. "Then I can be her boyfriend—you know, someday when I'm the same age as her," he added. "Just kidding!"

Mr. Kawada glanced around the table and stood with sudden alarm. We count four people here. Four is very, very bad luck number." He spoke between his teeth. "Four . . . means death. So sorry, I go back to room now!" Bowing stiffly, he left quickly. ". . . means death."

At the word *death*, Stewie frowned. They watched Mr. Kawada leave.

The three of them walked quietly toward the carousel. When Stewie broke the silence, Hetty and Morgan turned to him. He sounded serious.

"You know, Ben yells at his lawyer a lot. It's always stuff like, 'Stop telling me what I can't do!' He says the kind of stuff that should have got his mouth washed out with soap. One time he said, 'Then fix it so I *can* get away with it!' Ben figures I don't count, so he didn't know I was listening. Then he threw a shoe at me and said I'd better not tell. I was scared, but maybe I should have told Mom anyhow. She'd know all about what's right. Is that an ethics kind of thing?"

Morgan said it was, but he felt it was none of his business. He cleared his throat, and Hetty coughed, attempting to change the subject.

Playing the Part

By the time they got to the children's playroom, the ship was rocking more than before. One frazzled mother who was quite green in the face tried to lure her children back to their room. But the youngsters clung to the horses they were riding, unwilling to leave.

After trying reason and bribery, she gave up. Would Hetty and Morgan be willing to watch her boys in the playroom for a while? She was going to be sick and hadn't the strength to cope with them.

Hetty surprised Morgan with her enthusiasm for wiping noses and settling minor skirmishes. She enlisted Stewie, who was willing to help alert them to any property damage or bodily harm. As the number of parents thinned out, more unsupervised children joined them.

Morgan would have liked to make the marionettes perform in the raised puppet theater; however, they were locked up. Next to the hopscotch court, Hetty found some beanbags for him to juggle. Soon he was teaching a gathering of five- and six-year-olds about juggling and how to perform simple magic tricks.

Meanwhile, Hetty's lap was full of the younger ones. Together they sang songs and made up nonsense words.

Hours later, when the parents dribbled back, the children were as reluctant to leave as before. They begged to hear more tales of adventure from Morgan or to play games with Hetty. A delicate toddler with bouncy red curls tightened her arms around Morgan's neck. "Mine!" she announced.

A quiet couple came from the corner where they had sat watching. "You're the honeymoon couple, aren't you? Your children are going to be very lucky someday."

"That's kind of you," said Hetty. "My husband does have a way with young people. He raised his little sister."

The children covered Hetty's cheeks with tiny wet kisses, and Morgan felt her happiness. If only such contentment could last forever! He wanted to hold her close and protect her from hurt—to preserve the radiant joy he saw in her now.

Suddenly, her eyes had a faraway look, and he could think only of her sorrow. She would always have a hole in her heart where children ought to be. He could never fill the void. He didn't care if Stewie thought they were being "all stupid and mushy." Morgan wanted to provide whatever comfort Hetty might need. But when the playroom was empty, Hetty stood tall and seemed ready to leave. Stewie said he had fun helping, and he was sure the magic tricks he learned would come in handy. He left to see if Troy wanted to play ping pong.

On the way to their room, they were tossed from one side of the corridor to the other. Morgan said he felt rather queasy, and the nap Hetty suggested sounded appealing.

She fluffed his pillow and said, "We have two stainless steel wastebaskets, in case we need to use them." She placed a cool washcloth over his forehead and asked if he wanted to take a Dramamine for his nausea. Attempting a weak smile, he turned it down, saying it wouldn't keep the ship from rocking.

He was right about that. The ship continued to roll rhythmically from side to side. Though he encouraged Hetty to go to the dining room, she didn't mind missing a meal. Instead she chose to stay with him until he felt better.

"I didn't want you to see me like this," he said.

Morgan thought of her glowing countenance earlier. Under her influence, the playroom had assumed a sweet and rare atmosphere of harmony.

Nothing would give Hetty more joy than a child of her own. I put her in an agonizing position. How could I have been so thoughtless? Hetty had to watch me play the part of a father. She must never know how much I loved every minute of it.

Suddenly, he thought of the telegram.

I should have found a better place to hide it. At least she wasn't suspicious. I admire that quality in her character—her respect for privacy. But I'm afraid if she picks up the Bible, she'll find it. Meanwhile, there's nothing I can do about it.

Morgan's skin turned a chalky white, and he felt cold and clammy all over. Hetty held the wastebasket for him. When nausea overcame him, he leaned his head over it just in time.

"I'm sorry," he gasped. "I'll empty it in a minute." This was not exactly how he had planned to cheer his wife.

For a time, he dozed off, then awakened to feel Hetty's hand on his chest.

Her voice was pensive and gentle, as if trying not to wake him. "I love you, Morgan," she whispered. Her hair brushed his ear like an angel's wing. He lay still so she wouldn't leave, and once again he fell asleep.

When he awoke, Hetty was sleeping beside him. She had emptied the contents of the wastebasket and covered him with a light blanket. He felt better now.

She must have opened the balcony door a crack before falling asleep. The fresh sea breeze lifted her pale hair, soft as sea foam. Fascinated, he watched a moment.

Then with slow, stealthy movements, he rose unnoticed. It seemed almost like playing pick-up sticks with his sister. He had been clever at removing his sticks without disturbing the rest of the pile, though he usually allowed her to win.

Watching to be sure Hetty remained asleep, Morgan slowly opened the drawer and retrieved the telegram from under the Bible.

Bitter Salt

After the steady rolling motion of the ship had rocked Hetty to sleep, her thoughts drifted seamlessly into a dream:

She was standing at the starboard bow. Beside her, Morgan's powerful body held firm against the thundering waves, and he lifted her high. The sea was love, and the glory of the sea was theirs alone. Hetty licked the salt from her lips, and it tasted sweet.

Suddenly, the winds increased, and the tempest pounded against the port bow.

What was that ghostly object in the distance? Morgan appeared to know what it was. Quickly, he carried Hetty aft. Setting her down, he left her with instructions to hold fast to the poop deck taffrail.

His words bewildered her. Hoping the coarse rope overhead might be the taffrail, she clung to it with numb and bleeding hands. A wall of water bashed against her, washing her along the deck like so much flotsam.

She thought surely Morgan would notice and discover her peril, but his attention was on the ghostly ship that was rapidly gaining on them. It broke through the fog to reveal a beautiful figurehead at the bow—a glorious woman with flowing hair, carved in wood.

It turned its head and fluttered its long eyelashes in Morgan's direction. It was Katrinka Wallace! But why was Morgan clenching a rope between his teeth? He dove into the sea. Hetty watched him through the seaweed that drooped across her face. Spent and weak, she trembled at the thought of losing him.

What was that thin, pleading voice she heard? "Help me! Help me, Morgan!" It was Katrinka heaving up and down between the swells. "My hero," she crooned, as Morgan struggled to reach her. "But do be careful not to lose my dainty size-five shoes from Neiman Marcus." Her arms tightened around his neck, and she displayed her dimples just for him. "I knew you'd save me, Honeybun!"

"Well," he gasped. "I could see you just got a manicure, and I didn't want you to chip your nails." Morgan carried her shapely form up the rope ladder and onto the deck.

Katrinka powdered her nose. "You needed me, didn't you, sweetheart? Hetty doesn't know how to entertain children, bless her heart!"

"Oh . . . I seem to have misplaced Hetty."

He looked around absently. "Oh . . . I seem to have misplaced Hetty." When he found her, Morgan gathered her in his arms with no regard for the blood and wet seaweed on her person. He wiped her nose with his handkerchief and patted her on the head.

Hetty didn't have the strength to tell him someday her brilliant legal mind would dazzle him and his Harvard classmates. They would have to address her as "Your Honor." And nobody would dare pat her on the head.

At the carousel, Katrinka arranged herself upon a seahorse, after selecting one with a saddle that matched her pink scarf. She addressed the multitude of her admirers, granting permission for anyone who wished to vomit to do so discreetly. "However," she added, "please be so kind as to keep the children at a distance. I hate their sticky little fingers!"

With each revolution, Katrinka leaned out to try catching the brass ring, but it stayed out of reach. In frustration, she said, "Morgan, darling, is this silly little ring the best you could do for your wife? The diamond you gave me was so spectacular!"

Hetty looked down at her left hand. Her wedding ring was missing from her finger! That must be the one Katrinka was trying to grab. She must get on the carousel immediately and retrieve it herself.

But between her and the carousel, the bare frame of a doorway stood in her way. The two sides of it were marked in inches, and the measurements continued upward to meet a beam across the top. A loudspeaker blared out the warning: "To ride the carousel, a person or persons must fit through this opening. Tall, shapeless, unattractive persons need not apply."

Eligible or not, Hetty knew she must try. When she bent over at the waist to pass through the frame, it became tighter and tighter. Soon she became hopelessly wedged in the opening. Falling forward on her face, she pulled it crashing down around her.

Katrinka glanced in her direction and whispered to Morgan, "You poor dear. Once upon a time, when you and I were bespoke, we made such a gorgeous couple! And I could have given you all the sticky-fingered, runny-nosed little children you wanted." Her perfect, pearly-white teeth grew longer and sharper as she spoke.

Morgan looked forlorn. "I know." He glanced down at the doorframe and sighed. "Hetty may not be much to look at, but I admire the loving attitude she has toward all mankind."

Standing over the tangled figure of skin and bones, he tried to extricate Hetty from the splintered lumber. Her bottom waved in the air, and he pulled her dress down to cover her underwear.

The dead fish in her hair were beginning to smell, but he leaned over to whisper in her ear. "Don't mind Katrinka. She means well."

Convulsed with rage, Hetty hissed, "No, Morgan. She does not." The salt on her lips was bitter.

Hetty struggled to give voice to her hatred. Though the words remained caught in her throat, her ugly thoughts could not be contained. They seemed to echo, growing louder and more hideous with each repetition.

Morgan could hear her hateful thoughts, and a profound sadness showed in the depth of his eyes. His disappointment was more than Hetty could bear. She covered her face with her hands. In agony, she moaned aloud.

Hetty was jolted from sleep by her own voice. "Oh!" She blinked and was relieved to look up into Morgan's kindly eyes. "Did I sleep too long?"

"Not at all." He smiled. "You needed it."

Cowardice

When arriving at the breakfast table, Hetty and Morgan found Stewie examining his soft-boiled egg. He asked Troy, "What if they forgot to cook it, and then I opened it, and then this chicken popped out, then it hopped around on everybody's plates and stuff?"

Sophie suggested he sit up straight. This effectively reminded Stewie a gentleman should not allow his chicken to frolic unattended on the tabletop. He opened the eggshell, then sighed, as if to express disappointment that it contained neither more nor less than an egg.

When Stewie received his mother's permission to go swimming, he ran off to look for his bathing suit with the spaceships on it.

When breakfast was over, Hetty and Morgan walked along the deck. The sky was still gray and gloomy, but the sea was quieter today. She and Morgan sat on deck chairs to read and watch the circling gulls. They were alone.

Morgan had checked out a magazine about the president of France. Charles de Gaulle had been elected by a huge majority the previous year. Already his Fifth Republic was enacting economic measures to adversely impact American business.

Hetty had found a copy of *A Tale of Two Cities* in the library. She had read it in high school. But now that she and Morgan were going to Paris, the French Revolution once again seemed to deserve attention.

She read only as far as the first page before closing the book. *It was the best of times, it was the worst of times . . .*

Hetty didn't want to read about the worst of times. "Morgan, I wonder why knots isn't spelled n-a-u-t-s, like with nautical miles."

"Because they used to tell speed by attaching a chip log to a reel. They'd tie knots along the reel, then drop the log overboard and count the number of knots going through their hands in a minute."

"How fast do you think we're going?"

"Top speed is 31.69 knots, going east. We'd be doing less than that. So . . . I'm guessing about 33 miles an hour." Morgan's mind seemed to be somewhat distracted during his explanation. Suddenly, he said, "I know who he is!"

"Who?"

"Ben Benutto. I thought I'd heard of him. He's in the salvaging business. He buys ships after they've been scrapped. He's been mixed up in some shady deals. Either there were ships he sank that weren't ready to retire or he salvaged ships before the owners could find them. I can't remember exactly. Maybe some Mafia connection?" Morgan spoke quietly as if asking himself the question. "If Ben has government contracts, this may be important to know. In fact, it's possible Stewie knows too much about him, and that's why he wants to send him away."

Hetty said, "Maybe he's sending him away to Phillips Exeter to give him the education his mother couldn't afford. We know he wants to help Sophie."

"Yes, but she seems almost afraid of him."

"Or," Hetty said, "beholden to him?"

"You mean because she may *want* Stewie in a boarding school?"

"It's possible. But that separation might be a mistake. We know it was for . . . you know, some people."

Morgan sent a smile in her direction. "Feel free to say the name 'Katrinka.'"

Hetty blushed. She hadn't meant her discomfort to be so obvious. "Yes . . . that is, I know boarding school was wrong for Katrinka. But I'm sure her father thought it was best."

Morgan rolled the magazine. "It's only because Phil was a dwarf. He thought it would be socially awkward for her, living at home with him. They missed each other terribly."

"I'm glad he was lonely enough to take *you* in as much as he did."

"Yes, Phil was like a father to me." Morgan paused as if remembering good times with Phil—his coaching as a clown, or his advice as a circus executive. "Phil never stopped believing in my dad. He saw the best in him. Just like you did."

Hetty nodded. "The good wasn't hard to see. Max and Mimi are important to me now. And not just because they're your parents."

Morgan put down the magazine. "You amaze me, Hetty—being so understanding about the money."

Hetty leaned back in the chair and considered her answer. "I just hope you never regret what you lost."

He shook his head. "I'm the big-time winner. I got you."

Hetty couldn't think of anything to say, so Morgan filled in the silence. "I'll be able to support you comfortably," he said, "with a job in the conglomerate—whether circus or cosmetics," he said. "And it's a good arrangement, practicing law with your papa. It's good of Dan to forgive my time out of the office."

"He's excited to have you. He's already put your name up in gold letters. *Lawrence and Morganthal, Attorneys at Law.*" Hetty had been hoping her name could be up there too, but she would have to wait for the right opportunity to mention it.

Katrinka was the one who was losing the most, but Hetty didn't want to bring up her name again.

She didn't have to. Morgan said, "Katrinka's going to be fine. My parents will let her stay on in the gatehouse. She'll love living on their estate. You know that portrait of Dad and Phil?" he added. "The big one Dad had commissioned?"

Among the hundreds of paintings, Hetty couldn't remember any particular one.

"They're wearing their clown suits in it," he said. "Now it's in the gatehouse. Dad gave it to Katrinka when Phil died."

Would Katrinka always be a part of their lives? An oppressive feeling smothered Hetty. She pictured Katrinka standing at the kitchen window, watching Max and Mimi Morganthal drive off in their Lamborghini.

Hetty had to know something. "Is she . . . is Katrinka coming here on business?"

"While we're on our honeymoon?" Morgan laughed as if the idea was completely outlandish, but he didn't say *no*.

A seagull landed on the railing and held Morgan's attention for a moment. "Dad wants Katrinka to be the new face of our cosmetics. Actually, the CEO."

Hetty tilted her head. Her expression was meant to invite Morgan's opinion on the matter, which he gave.

"She's rather, what should I say, assertive? That's . . . different in a woman. Maybe Joseph Ostler will come back from Australia and she'll be safely married."

"What do you mean by safely married?" asked Hetty. "Even if she marries Joseph, she could be effective in the job. As for being assertive, isn't that a reasonable quality for a CEO? You wouldn't mind if a *man* was assertive, would you? Or even pushy."

"That's not the same. There are just some things men are better suited for. There weren't any women in my law school. Probably because it wasn't logical to admit them."

Hetty knew Morgan was sending her a message: he remembered she had applied to law school and hoped she would decide against going.

The seagull glowered in their direction and left a large dropping on the deck.

It couldn't be a worse time to discuss law school. But Hetty was sure if she waited, Morgan would look back on this moment as an example of her cowardice.

Better to be pushy than cowardly, she thought.

Just as she prepared to speak, Morgan said, "About Ben, he's quite likeable. A man can change. I know that's your attitude, and it's rubbing off on me. See how strong your influence is? And you're not even being assertive."

Hetty tried not to look at the bird dropping.

She had hoped someday Morgan would take the initiative and ask if she had been accepted to law school. But for now, the chances of that seemed remote.

Maybe a short stroll would give her the courage to speak up. Warming her hands in her pockets against the damp chill, she walked with the purpose of clearing her mind.

In the distance, she saw the lady she had been noticing for the last two days. She was sitting alone as before, finishing a sack lunch.

Why did she never go to the dining room? First it was cheese and crackers, and yesterday a can of juice and a sandwich. Maybe she doesn't like people. But how could she dislike them enough to give up the amazing meals?

When Hetty returned, Morgan looked somber. After asking whether she had a nice walk, he picked up the magazine, as if to avoid further discussion.

CHAPTER FOUR

At What Cost?

"Morgan, I think . . . I think we need to talk."

"We just did."

Hetty smiled. "I'd call that our first fight."

"No," he said, "I know about fights. Dad left me black and blue."

"Call it an argument, then."

Morgan went back to his magazine, but he was holding it upside down. "I don't argue with my wife," he said. "If I did, I would absolutely refuse to admit it."

Hetty waited to see if he would turn the page.

"I can feel your eyes," he said. Soon, one corner of his mouth turned up. "I read faster upside down." They shared a short, uneasy laugh, and he turned to her. "So, what about this *fight*?"

"I just mean . . . my battle is with me, and yours is with you."

"How does that work?"

"Well, the fight I have with myself is between being what *you* want—a happy homebody—or being what would satisfy us both in the long run—a happy homemaker and lawyer."

He took a deep breath and looked at the angry sky. "So, who won?

"I don't see it as a game of winning or losing. I see it as an internal discussion each of us should have. The battle can't be *me* against *you*. One reason is that it might end in a Pyrrhic victory. And besides, you don't play fair."

"What do you mean I don't play fair?"

"You say nice things, and that's not fair."

"Really, Hetty . . . you expect me to understand this kind of fighting?"

"No, not really," she said. "But I'm glad if you're willing to hear me out."

"Of course."

She tried to relax while they both remained silent. Should they consider this some sort of truce? Hetty knew he was waiting, but she couldn't remember what she wanted to say. Maybe she wouldn't make a very good lawyer after all.

She closed her eyes, so she wouldn't have to look at the seagull dropping. Suppose someday she'd be standing before a judge and forget what she wanted to say.

She could only imagine:

"Mrs. Morganthal, please continue your argument."

"Thank you, Your Honor. May it please the court, Mr. Morganthal, counsel for the defense, is distracting me."

"I can understand your complaint, Mrs. Morganthal. The jury also finds him disturbingly handsome. However, as you are on the same side, I cannot declare a mistrial. Carry on. As you gain in experience, so to speak as it were, perhaps you will learn to concentrate."

"Yes, Your Honor. Thank you for your wisdom; however, when the said handsome distraction doesn't play fair . . ."

"Are you asking for a more severe sentence vis à vis the emoluments clause?"

"Well, Your Honor, the aforesaid gentleman, hereafter known as the Party of the First Part or some such, is not a foreign potentate. However, he has me entirely in his power, having given me everything I could ever hope for—meaning himself. If such generosity is not against the law, surely it ought to be."

There was a stir in the audience. The judge straightened his wig and pounded the gavel to demand more dignified behavior. "Order in the court! More decorum, you knaves! Just because Perry Mason lolls all over the bench, don't think I'll put up with your brouhaha." He cleaned his glasses with a corner of his robe. "So, what do you propose we do about the aforesaid distraction?"

Hetty said, "Inasmuch as there's not enough room for the three of us—I include my father, Mr. Lawrence—I think we should all be seated separately. As it is now, I'm unable to sit near Mr. Morganthal, I mean the Party of the First Part, without our sleeves touching."

The judge beckoned to the bailiff. In a whisper, he said, "Get three chairs for the defense."

"Huh?"

"I said, "Three chairs for the defense."

"Now?"

"Of course now, you duplicitous nincompoop."

The bailiff gave brief instructions to the jury, then spread his arms to lead them, as with a Sunday school choir.

The jury belted forth, "Three cheers for the defense! Hip, hip, hooray! Hip, hip, hooray! Hip, hip, hooray!"

So awe-inspiring it was, that the judge turned his wig around backwards and pumped his arms in triumph, saying, "Now that's how it's done! Eat your heart out, lower court!"

He cleared his throat to continue the proceedings. However, the chairs had been forgotten, and Hetty was forced to sit next to her beloved emolument. For a moment, she was overwhelmed with affection for him.

"Your Honor, he smells like a fresh mountain breeze, and his eyes are a deep blue with little flecks of brown that dance when he smiles. His dark eyebrows are serious but betray an intelligent sense of humor."

The judge waved the lace jabot that cascaded downward from his double chin. "That's enough, counselor. Perhaps I should say counselorette," he cackled. "Continue."

Upon gaining her composure, Hetty launched her argument: "Your Honor, even a child knows that according to international law, when riding in a car with friends and other personages, you're supposed to lay claim to your own section of the seat with a stripe of masking tape. The Party of the First Part claims ignorance of this time-honored rule."

"That's preposterous! I know the type—I doubt if he respects dibs, or frontsies and backsies." He honked his nose into a large red handkerchief. "What have you done to explain the rule to him?"

"Nothing, Your Honor."

"And why not?"

"Because I didn't want to. I also didn't want to put a stripe of masking tape down the middle of the bed. You see, he smells like a fresh mountain breeze, and his eyes are a deep blue with . . ."

"All right already!" The judge banged his gavel. "That will be all, Mrs. Morganthal! What did you expect, for heaven's sake! I mean, res ipsa loquitur!"

"Oh, but may I approach the bench?"

"Only if you don't have cooties."

At that, Mr. Morganthal stood. A hush fell over the court. His magnificent bearing and dignified demeanor dazzled the jury. Several women fainted upon viewing his dear countenance.

The judge asked, "What is it, Mr. Morganthal?"

"Your Honor, I object to your using the word cooties in connection with Mrs. Morganthal. Would you kindly strike it from the record?"

Hetty's eyes closed while she let the sound of Morgan's voice reverberate throughout the depths of her soul.

The judge stood and bowed deeply. "Certainly, Your Honor, I mean Mr. Morganthal. My sincere apologies." He shuffled some parchments and opened a scroll. "Let's see now, we were talking about fairness?" He turned to face Hetty, but she was still in her emolument-induced trance. "Listen up, Mrs. Morganthal! I mean don't be so spacy." He pounded his gavel. "Good grief, you have the rest of your life to spend in his thrall! I can't help you unless you give me your attention."

When Hetty's book hit the deck, it interrupted her reverie. "I'm sorry, Morgan. Where were we?"

"You were going to suggest a topic of discussion between me and myself."

"I don't really want to anymore."

"If I insist?"

Hetty bit her lower lip. "Maybe later?"

"We can't stop now, after just half a talk."

That sounded reasonable, so she began. Reluctantly at first.

"We both know I applied to law school," she said. "So, I'm guessing there are two ideas fighting inside you. I suppose the first is to wish it never happened or to pretend you've forgotten about it." Hetty didn't dare look at Morgan. If she did, she would lose her courage. "I think the second," she said, "is to make me feel like you'll love me more if I'm submissive, and therefore ill-equipped to be an attorney."

Her hands were trembling. "But," she said, "that's not . . . I mean, that wouldn't be playing fair." The honesty of this outpouring left Hetty feeling weak, but she continued just the same. "I think you've been fighting with yourself to decide which one of those plans will work."

The seagull dropping spread on the damp deck. She stared at it and supposed Morgan was doing the same.

With a jerk, Morgan rose from the deck chair to face the wind. He avoided the spreading mess and walked to the railing. Hetty could see the back of his neck and one ear. They were a deep red, and he clenched the muscles of his jaw.

Hetty stared at the gray madness of the empty sea. The gloom smothered her with a sickening, briny scent. Earlier, the gulls had circled overhead, laughing at her. Now they were nowhere to be seen.

Morgan made a fist.

More than once she had seen him with a black eye. What had he done to his *father* in return? Until now, she never thought to wonder how he might resolve a conflict. Was he preparing to confront her?

Hetty's hands made a few short, nervous flutters to smooth her skirt. Eyes wide with apprehension, she breathed rapidly.

She remembered her mother saying, *you need to deal with disagreements before you're married. It's an important way to learn about each other.* But they never had.

Hetty saw the tension in the muscles of his back. Leaning his forearms on the railing, he cracked his knuckles.

Morgan turned toward her with a dark look, and her mouth went dry. Oblivious to the mess underfoot, he moved closer.

As he did, someone called out to get their attention. It was Stewie. The rest of the group followed close behind. Hetty had forgotten the tour was scheduled for this hour. She greeted their cheerfulness with a stiff wave. Maybe having people around would give her time to think. But how could she conceal the boiling confusion of her thoughts?

What had she done? For now, she must pretend nothing had happened. She had told Morgan her honest feelings. But at what cost?

The Tour

The group moved to the bridge in a cluster. They huddled in their jackets until the Chief Officer was ready to take them on a tour.

Troy and Ben tried to engage Morgan in conversation, but he responded with peculiar silence and a blank stare.

Hetty's mind was numb. Earlier, she had expressed curiosity about the ship. But now she hadn't the energy to hear details. She imagined herself a sluggish turtle withdrawing into its shell.

Following their tour, the group of eight became somewhat fluid in their organization. Some remained with the Chief Officer, to ask more questions. Sophie wandered between Ben and wherever he left his cane. Mr. Kawada showed everyone his new Nikon camera, then flitted here and there taking photographs. He asked if Hetty would take a picture of Miko and him before a row of tenders. They took another with a smokestack in the background.

When Miko ambled away out of hearing, her father approached Hetty about a personal matter. "Before wife die, is raise Miko and talk very wise words together." He shook his head. "Now no wife. No mother for Miko, but maybe you can help, same like mother. Always, Miko cry in cabin. Crying not Japanese way. But Miko is Nisei—American girl. Maybe you understand how to make American girl Miko stop crying and marry nice Japanese boy?"

"I . . . I don't know . . ."

He must have thought she meant *yes*, so he bowed and said, "Thank you," Mrs. Moruganutaru.

"Please, will you call me Hetty?"

He smiled. "Ah, yes. More easy to say."

Whatever Mr. Kawada had in mind, she would have to learn about it later. Meanwhile Hetty stood staring at nothing. The movement of Miko nearby was a blur of no importance.

She sensed Morgan standing alone, not too far away. She could feel him.

She supposed the hole in her heart was of her own making. Or was it Morgan's? Did she really know him? Some unknown something was now lost, but she couldn't be sure what it was.

Was Mr. Kawada stretching over the railing for something? Maybe his camera. It had been attached to some part of his apparel—maybe his suspenders. Now it dangled just out of reach, blowing in the wind. But he would get it with no trouble. Peering from under his arm, he glanced at Hetty and grinned. Aha!" he said. She laughed and turned away.

Without warning, the ship lurched.

Hetty lost her balance, lunging against the railing. Mr. Kawada was no longer there but hung over the water by the strap of his camera. There was no time to think. Quickly, Hetty straddled the railing, giving Mr. Kawada something more solid to grab. He clung to her leg with both arms and bellowed for someone to save them. Hetty thought of his earlier words. *Four means death.*

Help came with breathtaking speed. Morgan gripped Hetty around the waist with one arm and pulled Mr. Kawada to safety with the other. Whether from the near casualty, or because of Morgan's rescue, the pounding of her heart left Hetty breathless.

When Miko gained her balance, she cried, "Oto-san!" Standing with her father, she heard his outpouring of gratitude to Morgan.

"No, no," Morgan insisted. "It was my wife." Mr. Kawada's face colored, and he seemed to purposely ignore Hetty.

Miko took Hetty aside. "Are you all right? Please believe I'm most grateful for what you did. And I need to explain something. For a Japanese man, it's hard enough being indebted to a man. So, to owe his life to a woman—can you understand how such a thing would be . . . humiliating?"

"Of course," said Hetty. "There's no reason to mention it again. I'm sure no one else saw."

"Thank you . . . thank you again." When Miko didn't leave her side, Hetty waited to hear what else she had to say. "Hetty, I understand my father's customs. But they aren't mine. I wonder . . . I'm hoping you can help me. He doesn't understand it's different for me. Maybe you could explain how it is here."

"I . . . I don't know," said Hetty.

Miko continued and spoke rapidly. "My boyfriend John is Nisei too, but his parents have accepted the American ways completely."

Hetty felt drained and exhausted. "Nisei?" she asked. "That means Japanese American?"

"Yes," Miko said, "second generation. My parents' marriage was arranged, and they didn't have any problem with that."

Hetty was desperate to rest before facing Morgan. After promising Miko they would talk, she excused herself.

Too Late Now

Hetty returned to their room. They must have left the blinds closed when they went to breakfast, and she would keep them that way. The darkness was welcome. Maybe she could collect her thoughts before Morgan's arrival.

Feeling for the easy chair, she sat, pulling her skirt forward. Its hem dangled around her ankles. Apparently, it had ripped on the railing.

When is he coming? Hetty's breathing slowed, but the confusion of her thoughts did not.

Mr. Kawada said the number four means death.

A voice startled her. "You've made a mistake." It was Morgan, and his voice was raspy. "It's too late now," he said.

Muffling her shock, she looked for him, but her eyes were not used to the dark. He sounded wooden and mechanical.

"You didn't know me, did you?" he said.

Holding her breath, she waited. What answer was he expecting? Hetty was still for what seemed an eternity.

Again, came his voice. "Know what you did?" he said. "You showed me what I am inside, and it wasn't a pretty picture."

Where was he going with this? She could see a little better now. He was slumped over in the other chair. "You read my mind," he said. "I've been at war with myself ever since."

"Oh?"

Now she understood his rage. It was all inside. She said, "Then . . . then what are you thinking now?"

The silence that followed puzzled Hetty. She heard only the creaking of the ship.

"Please give me time," he said. "I need to get used to your going to law school."

Now she could see him. He looked worn-down and haggard. Why had she been afraid?

He leaned forward. "You know what I've always pictured? I could see you waiting for me to come home from the office—wearing a white apron. Singing in the kitchen while we watch you bake cookies."

"We, Morgan? That's what I want, too. I just can't have it."

He stood and pulled her close. "Forgive me."

Hetty pressed her forehead against his. "It was no mistake marrying you. I'd do it all again." She kissed his cheek. "And I'm glad it's too late now."

He held her away from him. "We should have had this conversation before we married. Hetty . . . whenever we have differences, let's talk."

"Yes." She sat on the bed. "And that means no secrets too, doesn't it?"

She waited for him to agree. Instead, he sat a short distance from her and said, "People have misunderstandings even when they mean well. It's easy to misinterpret words."

"I know. Remember the time you took Melinda and me to your school fair? I was twelve at the time. I waited at the booth where they were showing how to change a tire, but the instructor turned me away. He said, 'But you're a girl!' Then you came to my defense. You said, 'She most certainly is not!' That's when I decided Papa's Forest Service boots weren't very feminine."

"Oh, no!" he said. "I was already an oaf at sixteen."

"No, you were a hero to me. I learned to change a tire because of you. But you hardly ever saw me wear those boots again."

Hetty wanted to sit closer, but sensed Morgan must have his reasons for staying at a distance.

Of course, he was right. When a problem starts with words, it takes words to untangled it. She remembered once struggling to undo a rope that seemed hopelessly knotted. Eventually her fingers undid the tangles. But it would have been ludicrous to try undoing them with a kiss.

The rocking motion felt pleasant to her now. She changed the subject. "Miko and her father have both talked to me about a sensitive matter. He's arranged a marriage for her, but she'd rather make her own choice."

Morgan was quiet a moment. Was he thinking of the arrangement his parents made for him to marry Katrinka?

"Interesting," he said. "Miko's way might seem best to us, but sometimes I think parents choose more wisely."

Hetty opened the blinds to see what damage she had done to her skirt.

"We'll get you a new one," he said.

"It's all right. I'll repair it and save the money."

"You worry too much." He reached behind her ear and produced a magic quarter. "See how easy it is?"

She laughed at the trick but said nothing. Already she was keeping a secret from him. His casual attitude toward money worried her.

Lady Mondegreen

"I know you can help them work it out," Morgan said. "Miko and her father, that is. No one could do it better."

Hetty was surprised. Was he implying she'd make a good lawyer?

"I wonder if I can," she said. "You'll remember even their meaning for the word *yes* confused me."

Morgan chuckled. "English doesn't always make sense either. Take the word *useness,* for instance."

"What's useness?"

"It's a word I heard Phil use. Before every meal, when he said grace, he'd say, 'Bless this food to our useness to thy service.' I puzzled over that for years. He was actually saying, 'Bless this food to our use and us to thy service.'"

Hetty clapped her hands. "What fun! That's a Mondegreen!"

"A What?"

"A Mondegreen. It's like in the "Star-Spangled Banner" where it says *José, can you see by the donzerly light?*

"Oh, yes!" he laughed. "And like the wooden shoe song. You know—it starts out, *Mares eat oats* and ends with *a kid'll eat ivy too, wooden shoe?"*

Their laughter made it hard to talk, but she said, "I learned about Mondegreens in a magazine. It was in an essay by a woman named Wright. When she was little, her mother read her an old ballad called "The Bonnie Earl o' Moray." She thought it said *They hae slain the Earl o' Moray and Lady Mondegreen.* But the real words were: *They hae slain the Earl o' Moray and laid him on the green.*

"Her essay described the devotion of the lovers dying together. But when she learned the real words, she was furious to think the poor man died alone with no Lady Mondegreen to hold his hand. Anyway, now she wants *Mondegreen* to become an accepted term."

"I'd accept it," Morgan said, "wooden shoe?"

Their laughter was slow to subside.

Though there were decisions yet to be made, Hetty felt giddy with relief and a renewed affection for her husband.

Perplexing

Lunch was served on the Promenade deck. On their way there, Morgan stopped, saying he remembered unfinished business and would have to return to the room.

Hetty went on alone and found the table half empty when she arrived.

It was easy to see Troy was developing a bond with Stewie. Hetty's own longing to be a parent made that sentiment easy to recognize in others. But for some reason, Sophie was quite reserved around him. Why did she seem to warm to Troy and, at the same time, discourage his friendship so pointedly?

When Stewie left to go swimming, Sophie gathered rolls and jam for Ben. She opened a small bag she had brought for that purpose.

"Let me carry it for you," Troy said.

"Oh . . . thank you . . . Hetty, will you come too?"

When the threesome arrived at Ben's door, Hetty heard him shuffling things around before inviting Sophie to open it.

Apparently, he had been waiting with a suggestion. "I may want Troy to paint my portrait," he said. "I could use a big oil to the right of my desk. You decide, Sophie. Get him to show you some samples." He looked through the opening at Troy. "Do you have something she can see?"

"Yes. I mean no. That is . . . not right now. I'm about to go see a landscape in the Long Gallery."

Ben waved them all away. "Go see it. Take Sophie." He limped to the bed, and they left.

Morgan was waiting back in the room. When Hetty arrived, he stood. He had found something to eat, but mostly he had been thinking about Ben. He sat on the bed, and before long he was deep in thought. Leaning forward, he brushed his knuckles against his chin.

It was a small gesture, but Hetty felt a breathless excitement for no reason. The thrill of belonging to him washed over her with an exquisite sweetness. Because he appeared preoccupied, she remained standing. With dubious success, she tried to quell her sentiments.

Was love meant to be this way? Maybe it would always be a sweet unfulfilled longing. A desire to give more than possible. Perhaps it meant almost understanding each other, but not quite. Maybe it was simply laughing together. One thing was sure. It meant she would always care about him. Beyond all dimensions. Longer than time.

Her thoughts continued.

Maybe you shouldn't be everything to me. Is it wrong to love you so much? I'm like the empty shell of a hermit crab— lifeless without you. The one way I feel complete is when we're united.

Will I feel this way forever? Maybe I need to feel complete when I'm alone.

I can imagine you coming home after a day full of fascinating challenges. You'll be defending our nation's downtrodden citizens and making the world a better place. I want to be a part of it. Can't we work side by side?"

Morgan reached out his hand, and Hetty welcomed the invitation to sit with him. He was still talking about Ben.

"If he's trying to marry Sophie," he said, "all the more reason to check him out. But I'm not sure how."

Hetty was finding she had another secret to keep from Morgan: she wasn't much interested in discussing Ben at the moment. She was more intrigued by the way Morgan's lips slid across his white teeth, then closed together at the end of each sentence. She rested her left elbow on her knee to watch.

From that vantage point she could also look up his nose. The black hairs in his left nostril were a marvelous new discovery! This delightful new familiarity with his nose gave her almost a sense of ownership. Perhaps Lewis and Clark had a similar relationship with the land they discovered!

She put her head on Morgan's shoulder. "Should we explore the ship while you think about it?"

Hetty carried along the book to be returned, as the library was the first place they wanted to visit. Morgan agreed the rich wooden panels smelled like her Papa's law office. Inside the door, they were pleased to see Troy and Sophie whispering at one of the tables. The two of them were conversing about the portraits in a large album, too busy to notice anyone.

Hetty whispered, "Troy's showing her his portfolio. Ben might commission a portrait of himself."

"We should see it too. I may want a painting of you while we're on our honeymoon."

"Shouldn't we wait? Stewie would want us to leave them alone."

As they turned to leave, Sophie noticed them and smiled. "You need to see these." She indicated two empty chairs. Troy's absolutely brilliant!"

But Troy appeared startled, as if caught off guard. Standing quickly, he snapped shut his portfolio. "I wouldn't want to bore you." His lips were firm, and he left immediately.

Such odd behavior left Sophie looking puzzled, and there was nothing to say about the awkwardness.

Walking back to their room, Morgan tried to make light of the encounter. "It was like the toothpaste ad. People scatter when the guy with halitosis comes along. We may as well go back to the room. I know who to ask about Ben. I'll get more facts first, then I'll call Commander Slubbet.

Slubbet. Hetty felt revulsion at the name. Folding her arms tight, she moved with uncertain, mincing steps. Why Commander Slubbet? The memory of him sickened her.

CHAPTER FIVE

Courtesy of Bugs Bunny

Hetty got ready for dinner early. Morgan suggested she go on ahead without him. He would join her soon. She knew black-tie affairs required a lot of complicated trappings for a man. Plus, he probably planned to shave again.

Hetty was in no particular rush to get to the dining hall without him. Why not explore some of the rooms she hadn't seen yet? She peeked into a cavernous entertainment room. The slow creaking of the ship's bones echoed across the highly polished floor, increasing its eerie magnificence. After just one more door, she would save others to explore later with Morgan.

Behind the next door, Hetty saw a beautiful woman with red hair and a purple scarf standing on a stage. She kept telling a man, "Nobody else would object." The man, who stood below the stage, looked like Morgan. But it couldn't be. Morgan said he was going back to their stateroom.

In spite of her begging, the man was firmly refusing something.

The sack lunch lady was on Hetty's mind. She wondered if the woman would show up at dinner tonight or if she was hiding in her usual place.

No, she wasn't there. Suddenly, a new thought occurred to her. Maybe the woman didn't know meals were included in the price of the trip! With only two full days left on the ship, Hetty felt an urgency to find her wherever she might be.

After almost giving up her search, there she came, and Hetty began to enact a plan. When she was settled in her deckchair, Hetty approached and introduced herself.

"Do you mind if I wait with you? I'm new to this kind of travel, and I don't think it's quite time for dinner yet."

"No problem."

Hetty began again. "Thank you. This is my first time. I'm so new to this I didn't even realize the food comes free with the trip!"

The woman placed her sack stealthily under her seat and appeared more interested than before. Hetty smiled and continued with a new idea. "My husband is back in the room. If it wouldn't be too much trouble, I'd rather have someone to walk in with. Besides, we have an extra space at our table." Hetty wasn't really sure about that, but decided if Ben should come, they could find her another chair.

"Well then," said the woman, "my name is Joan. I'll join you, if it would put you more at ease."

When they arrived at the table, Hetty was relieved it was as she had said—Morgan was late. Sophie said Ben didn't feel well and wouldn't be coming at all. Just for this meal, the steward asked if they would mind sitting at a table near the aisle. Aside from that, dinner went as usual. Joan appeared almost starry-eyed at the feast and seemed to enjoy the company.

Stewie was dazzled by all the formalwear and was generous with his compliments. He thought Morgan looked like Clark Kent except for not having glasses. He liked Hetty's dress a whole lot because her ribs didn't stick out as much as usual. He was especially complimentary about Troy's appearance, saying, "I think all men should have big noses like you. It makes you look real important."

"All men should have big noses like you."

Troy thanked him with sincerity, but Sophie fidgeted with her place setting until her son ran out of nice things to say.

After a dessert of crème brûlée, assorted cheeses and fruits were placed on the table. The lights dimmed, and a drumroll announced the program would begin. There were a few jokes and one tale about pirates and mermaids. Hetty thought the best part was when Morgan reached under the table to hold her hand.

The last entertainer surprised Hetty. It was the redheaded woman she had seen earlier. She wore the same purple scarf, but this time she was tightly wrapped in a long evening gown with a slit up the side. It was covered in gold sequins. The first songs were catchy enough that the audience clapped along. Then she sang "Come Softly to Me" and wandered into the audience. The spotlights followed as she flirted with a gentleman and ran her fingers through his hair. Hetty was embarrassed for the man, but the audience loved it.

Next the band played "Misty." The singer wandered around and sang unsuitably close to another gentleman. Suddenly she seemed to be making up some new words to the song. Her eyes were on Morgan, and she walked toward him singing, *"Walk my way, and a thousand violins begin to play."* Now the spotlights were on Morgan too. She kept singing, *"Morgan darling, at the sound of your hello, it's music I hear . . ."*

Morgan stood and moved into the aisle. What was he going to do? It looked like he was preparing to sing a duet with her! Hetty was confused. He couldn't sing, except for "Found a Peanut."

With a sudden flash, Morgan encased the woman in a black silk cubicle.

The lights flickered, and she was gone.

When the spotlights were trained on Morgan, he was sitting eating grapes, as if nothing had happened. Along with everyone in the dining hall, Hetty gasped.

Then the spotlights moved to show the singer on someone else's lap. To wild applause, she finished the song, *"I get misty the moment you're near."*

Stewie said, "That was cool! It started out super icky, I thought, you know . . ." He crossed his eyes and clutched his throat to demonstrate his reaction to ickiness.

The singer thanked the ladies and gentlemen of the audience. "And let's thank Morgan Morganthal!" There was more general applause, and she added, "Confidentially, I planned to sit on his lap till he got wind of it. He talked me into disappearing instead."

Blowing kisses around the room, she made her exit.

Joan whispered to Hetty, "I'm so glad we ran into each other. You didn't tell me your husband was in show business."

"He's not really, but he was raised in great part by a circus executive—Phil Wallace. Phil and Morgan's father were close friends." Joan wanted to know more, so Hetty said, "They had a clown partnership. My father-in-law, Max Morganthal, is rather tall. Phil was a dwarf. It was a very successful act, and Morgan learned a lot from Phil."

Later that evening when they were alone, Hetty asked Morgan how he did it.

"Oh, just vanishing cream, courtesy of Bugs Bunny."

"Thank you. Now I know." Hetty laughed. She respected professional secrecy and said no more.

"Any time," Morgan said. "But you're the magician, the way you got Joan to come. That was kind of you."

While Hetty brushed her hair, she thought about her charismatic husband. To her, it was no mystery that people were drawn to his goodness. Morgan claimed the attention he got was all because of his family's money, but she knew better. In a room of strangers, he always seemed to come out the leader.

Morgan watched while she wove her hair into two thick braids. His eyes were still on her as she tied the ends with a blue ribbon. When she was through, Morgan stood facing her. He cupped her cheeks in his hands.

"I love the way you are, Hetty. About tonight, you deserve more wholesome entertainment than that. I told her my lap was reserved for you. Still, I don't like things like that happening anywhere near you." He cradled Hetty's head against his chest. "I apologize. I should have known it would be as Stewie said— *icky*."

Hetty tightened her arms around his waist, and he stood holding her. Tears gathered in her eyes, but Morgan mustn't see them. Until she could blink them away, she stayed frozen in place.

Hetty thought of Slubbet and wished she could feel as pure as Morgan saw her.

The Fly

Maybe she wouldn't tell Morgan about Commander Slubbet. Long after he was asleep, Hetty was still thinking about her sickening experience. Would Morgan think her somehow tainted by it? She had been fourteen at the time.

She and Melinda Morganthal had both liked Susie Slubbet, a fellow student at Haxton Academy. So, when Susie asked her to spend the night at her house, Hetty was pleased to accept the invitation. Her home was out in the country. They lived on the campus of one of the finest prep schools in the area. The school had many acres of beautiful rolling hills enclosed within what seemed like miles of white fences.

Susie's father was headmaster, a prominent and well-respected man. But the most impressive thing to Hetty was that Morgan had graduated from that school the year before.

On a Friday night after dinner, Hetty arrived at Susie's house. On Saturday, the two of them explored the campus and never ran out of things to do. They studied together for a history exam and played Susie's latest piano piece with four hands, until discovering how late it was.

When Hetty asked if she could use their phone, Commander Slubbet came from nowhere and wondered if she was trying to get a ride from her parents. She said yes, they were planning on coming for her. He said he had to go in that direction anyway. Hetty wanted her Papa to pick her up because she wasn't very good at small talk. Especially with people she didn't know. Commander Slubbet insisted she should not bother them.

Hetty could even remember the rancid smell of his car. That evening came back to her in all its details. She wanted to smother all thoughts of it, but she could not, so vivid were her memories.

I was wondering what we could possibly talk about on a forty-minute ride. But I didn't have to talk at all. He turned on the radio and sang slightly off key. He swooped into each new phrase like he was trying to be Bing Crosby. Out of the corner of my eye I could tell he kept looking at me off and on. Kind of like he wanted me to say how great a singer he was.

I figured if I looked back at him just one time, he might decide he had succeeded in communicating and stop looking at me once and for all. So, I looked fast. His face disgusted me the way he was leering, and sweating, and crooning. I never looked again.

But he didn't stop glancing over at me. We were about halfway there when he turned off the radio and sang on his own.

"Vaya con dios, my darling, vaya con dios, my love."

Then he began at the beginning again. "Now the hacienda's dark the town is sleeping. Now the time has come to part, the time for weeping."

I guess that's the only verse he knew, but I wasn't going to tell him the words.

He put his right hand on my knee and I was too frightened to think sensibly. Was this really happening, and what did he mean by it? If I looked scared, would he do or say something worse? Maybe to convince me he could be comforting in a fatherly way?

I prayed with my eyes staring straight ahead.

A fly was squashed on the door of the glove compartment. Its insides were smeared next to its body, and the air coming through the vent made its wings vibrate. Maybe it drew attention to itself by flying around. If it had just stayed still in one place, would it still be alive?

I considered the fly and resolved to stay still in one place. Instead, I involuntarily moved my knees to the right and clamped them together. It was getting dark. I found myself clinging to the padded handle of the door and pressing against the paneling. I tried to make it look like I had moved away because I couldn't have seen out the window otherwise. I did it by craning my neck, as if fascinated by something that required my full attention, unfettered by his hand. Who was I fooling? And what point was there in pretending?

His hand was on my knee again, and stiffness was my only defense.

How much longer now? I was wearing a watch, but I didn't dare rotate my wrist to look at it.

My defense was exhausting me. I felt lightheaded and knew if I had to continue clenching all my muscles, soon I would be in danger of fainting.

I remember when it got too dark to see the fly. All I could do then was try to remember how it looked and keep my body stiff for protection. It almost felt like that fly had died just to help me to think. Is it foolish to be grateful for an insect?

I could hardly believe it when we pulled up to my front door! I said a stiff thank you and jumped out.

*Maybe the thought of Commander Slubbet will forever
make me feel unclean.*

Sleepless

The sea was more peaceful that night. The ship was through
creaking. Maybe they had experienced their one and only
rogue wave.

About four in the morning, Hetty could hear a whisper,
but she could barely make out what Morgan was saying.
"Hetty? Hetty, are you asleep?"

"No. I'm busy thinking."

"Me too. I need to go to the store.

"What do you need?"

A toothcomb," he said.

"Is there any such thing?"

"Sure. Bill Bailey had one. Remember the song, *Won't
you Come Home, Bill Bailey?* It says he left home *with nothing
but a fine toothcomb.* If that's all he took with him, it must be
better than a toothbrush. I want one too."

There was an explosion of laughter from both of them.
"It's taken me half the night to think of that one," he said.

"It's perfect!" she laughed.

The bed shook with their laughter. After a time, Morgan's
hand smoothed back her soft hair. "You can stop laughing
now and tell me what's on *your* mind."

Hetty put her hand in his and whispered, "I've been
thinking too." It had been about Slubbet.

But she felt quite clean now. Just from touching Morgan
and hearing him talk.

She was quiet a minute or two, then took a deep breath to
control her mirth. "One time," she said, "Mother was reading
a book. When she got to where it was describing a young
man, it said *he had feebly growing down on his chin.* We had no

idea what feebly could be—and why it was growing down on his chin."

"I don't get it. What *is* feebly?"

Hetty was laughing too hard to answer.

"Of course," he whispered, "the down was growing feebly, on his chin. What a difference a comma makes!"

"Why are we whispering?" said Hetty.

"So we won't wake each other up before the *donzerly* light.

"I really expected you to sleep soundly after your ordeal. You were amazing to think so fast. I'm not sure I understand Mr. Kawada's thinking. You saved his life, but the whole event seemed awkward for him. Was he embarrassed about the way he was hanging onto you?"

After hearing Hetty's explanation, Morgan understood. Reluctantly, he agreed to accept the credit in her place.

They both wondered about the fate of the new Nikon camera. Who might find it on the beach, twenty years from now? And how valuable might such a mysterious object be in a primitive society?

"Wars have started over lesser valuables," said Morgan, "but if I found it, no matter what it's worth, I'd use it to buy you as my bride."

"You say that now," said Hetty, "but what if we were in New Guinea? You'd be forced to give it away in a Kula exchange."

"What's that?"

"It's a ceremonial exchange system."

"Now you're talking war. It's got to be a barter economy, so I could trade the Nikon for *immediate* reward. I've already waited for you too long. On the other hand," he teased, "if the camera still works, I may hang onto it, instead."

"Then I would become so desperate," she said. "I'd make a counteroffer. What if I promised you a lifetime of washing your socks?" She assured him she would always sort his socks in daylight. That way, he wouldn't get to the office wearing one navy blue sock and one brown one.

Just as their bargain was resolved, the sun peeked through the curtains. Morgan kissed her on the neck. "Here's what I know," he said. "It's going to be hard to leave you in France."

They took turns yawning while Morgan stretched and put on his slippers.

Hetty wondered what perfume factories he would be visiting with Katrinka. *He's thinking I don't want to hear her name. But that would be better than pretending she's not coming.* Hetty decided not to think about it.

By the time she heard Morgan turn off the shower, Hetty was almost dressed for breakfast. She knocked on the door and called to him, "Ready when you are."

"Okay," came the answer. "I'll be out, soon as I comb my teeth and shave my feebly."

Last Breakfast Aboard

All nine people were at the breakfast table. No one wanted to miss a meal on the last day. Hetty could tell they all had mixed feelings about ending their adventures at sea. In the morning they would disembark in Southhampton.

Joan arrived and requested an extra place be set for her. Even Ben got there early wearing a bold plaid jacket. As Sophie turned his collar down, he told Troy he had decided against having a portrait of himself. The news appeared to disappoint Troy, until Ben explained what he really wanted was a portrait of Sophie. "Why should I have to look at my own mug, when I could look at a pretty face like hers? My villa's just a short daytrip from Paris. Why not join us there to paint her."

When Miko spoke to Hetty, her expression was mournful. "I wish we could have more time with you," she said.

Her father agreed. "Maybe Hetty and Morgan come see us in Tokyo." He looked at Morgan. "In Japan, I show you pearl business, to very much help cosmetics company."

"Wonderful," said Morgan. "I would appreciate that. Our new CEO says synthetics are cheaper, but I know real powdered pearls are better for the skin. I have a lot to learn about the business, but I don't want to use Bismuth oxychloride or pulverized fish scales."

"Maybe you bring CEO too! I am happy to show pearl business to him, same time."

"Thank you, but that won't be necessary. She's a woman. It should be enough to just tell Miss Wallace about it."

While Mr. Kawada continued talking with Morgan, Hetty spoke with Miko. "If you should decide to stay in Paris a while, I've had an idea."

Miko said she'd rather go straight to Tokyo to meet Kenzo and get it over with. Still, she listened to Hetty's suggestion.

Hetty said, "What if Kenzo came to France to meet you? It would be neutral territory. Neither of you would feel at a disadvantage. I'm sure your father wants what's best for you, and he'll be pleased if you seem eager to meet him. Who knows, maybe you'll like him."

Hetty could tell Mr. Kawada liked the idea too. The entire time Miko was speaking of it with him, he nodded at Hetty.

Meanwhile, Stewie had something to show Troy. "Want to see a neat trick? I can make my necktie melt," he said. "Pretend I just ate some Tabasco sauce." Then holding up the tip of his tie, he breathed on it while his thumb pulled down the lining. "No, wait," he added. Leaping from his seat, he went around the table and cupped his hands around Morgan's ear.

After Morgan whispered something in return, Stewie performed an improved version of the trick—this time with his thumb out of sight. Troy got everyone's attention, so they would see Stewie's trick before his tie melted clean away.

Joan had been puzzling over Morgan's job, so she asked him what cosmetics had to do with the circus. "Nothing really," he said, "Except they're the two Morganthal companies that need the most attention right now."

"What kind of attention?"

"All circuses have been struggling."

Ben asked, "Because of the Ringling Brothers and Barnum and Bailey disaster? I remember it was around 1944. It was still in the news as recently as six years ago. They had to pay about five million dollars to the families who filed claims."

"As you might imagine," said Morgan, "a lot of what we do is related to fire safety. That and of course reassuring the public."

"What about your cosmetics business?" Joan asked.

"That's been allowed to drift for years, but my father just decided to put a new face on it."

"Oh, yes, I heard you say you've got a new CEO. I'm impressed that you put a woman in that position. You must be expecting big things of her."

"Let's just say she'll be a new face. She's well known and should bring attention to our products."

Hetty volunteered that it was Katrinka Wallace—mostly to show Morgan she didn't mind saying the name.

"Oh, now I know you," said Joan. Then she was quiet. Hetty wondered if she was sorry she hadn't made the connection sooner or was embarrassed to mention it at all.

After breakfast Hetty and Morgan looked for Captain Bonnard and the chief officer. Even while thanking them for their kindness, Hetty was thinking of the earlier conversation.

They walked next to the railing. "Morgan . . . do you expect Katrinka to be just the face of the company? Nothing more than a figurehead?"

"Yes, she's willing to have her face out there representing the products. And I'm sure as long as the company does well, she'll be content with that."

"Are you sure she'd be satisfied with such a limited role?"

"She should be. It's not like a woman could really expect to lead the company in a meaningful way."

Hetty put her hand in Morgan's and stopped to face him. "Can you be sure?" His expression was so kindly, she felt certain he didn't intend to be unfair. "Don't you need to give her a chance to prove herself? Maybe as you work together."

Wouldn't this be the time for him to say he would be meeting Katrinka? Hetty waited for the answer that didn't come.

He took off his jacket to put around her shoulders. She was grateful that he noticed she was a little cold. Hetty gripped the railing.

She would *force* him to say it.

"I wonder," she said, "if by any chance she might be coming."

"Why would you think that?"

"Oh, maybe because . . . because it would give you a chance to see how well she can do the job."

Hetty wondered why Morgan didn't look the slightest bit guilty. Instead he said, "I don't want her here on our honeymoon." The way he looked at her conveyed wonder and respect. Morgan shook his head. Taking both her hands, he said, "But thank you for the suggestion."

Love muddled her head.

Katrinka was coming, and it was unbearable to go on thinking Morgan was keeping it from her. She would prefer to blame herself for it. She heard herself say, "If Katrinka comes, you could tour the perfume factories together." Her voice was weak and wobbly, but she continued. "It might be a good idea."

Right away she wanted to take it all back.

Please Wait

At lunch, Mr. Kawada looked happy. He told Hetty he had called Kenzo and would introduce Miko to him in Paris. "Thank you, Mrs. Hetty! Is very good idea." Everyone at the table seemed just as happy.

Hetty suggested they all discuss their favorite things to do. Stewie had a ready answer: He liked wrestling octopuses.

Ben glowered at him, but Troy threw his head back and laughed. "I hope you don't do that sort of thing too often."

"No, I just think about it a whole lot."

His mother laughed and said it was true, he really did.

Troy followed Stewie's example and mentioned something he hadn't done yet either. "My favorite thing to do is to paint Sophie's portrait."

Sophie blushed and changed the subject. "Hetty," she said, "What about you?"

Hetty glanced at Morgan. "Flying. Definitely soaring with Morgan in his glider. I've loved our time on the ocean, but there's nothing like floating in the air when it's quiet, with just the thermals to lift your wings."

Ben, who was in obvious pain, whispered to Morgan what his favorite thing would be. He declared it would be to take a pain pill and lie down. He finished eating his tomato aspic and drank from one of the goblets in front of his place. "Sophie," he said, "Don't wake me up for dinner. I didn't rest well last night."

After Ben left, the lively conversation continued. It was interrupted only by the brief absence of Sophie, who left to check on Ben. After finishing his flaming Baked Alaska, Stewie offered to take the key and check on Ben so his mother could pack their suitcases. They all separated to do the same.

While Hetty folded clothes, Morgan said, "I knew what you were going to say about gliding, and I'm glad you feel that way."

"It's not just the gliding, Morgan. It's doing it with *you*. I dream about it all the time."

"I'm glad. But dreaming isn't enough." His arms went around her. "I promise we'll be flying together before you know it."

Hetty decided the joy of being close to him was better than having the wind and the sky to hold her up. Her dream at that moment also included a kiss, a wish which he granted with all the zeal she had hoped for.

Lifting her, he swung her around, laughing. "My very own Mrs. Morganthal!" Setting her down, he kissed her again. "The more I see of the world," he said, "the more I love you."

When he said *the world*, was he referring to the forward behavior of the singer last night? Maybe the slit in her skirt? Whatever it was, Hetty felt it was right to keep her experience with Commander Slubbet to herself.

She knew not all good things can go on forever. But Morgan winked as if to say good things were merely on hold for the time being. Hetty sighed and watched him open his suitcase next to hers.

They planned out their last afternoon. There were more people to thank. Did that mean tipping them? Hetty marveled that Morgan knew how to do things like that.

"I'm almost packed," he said, "so I'll call the commander. By the way, Slubbet's the one who suggested me for the ethics committee. He'll be the chairman."

"The chairman?" Hetty froze in place.

Now with Slubbet on the Committee, she had no choice but to speak up. Morgan would need to know about him. But how should she start? "Oh, wait. Please . . ."

A heavy knock interrupted her. It was ship's security saying a possible crime had been committed, and an investigation was underway. With sincere apologies, the Morganthals must remain in their stateroom until further notice. Someone would bring them their dinner.

Under Suspicion

The officer made no further explanation, but after he left Morgan said, "Could be a robbery."

Hetty mentioned her first thought. "Or maybe murder on the high seas?"

Morgan laughed. "I'd say you have an active imagination."

They stood together looking out the window, and Hetty braced herself to talk to Morgan.

"You were . . . you were talking about Commander Slubbet"

She stopped to inspect the horizon. Maybe something there would give her courage to continue. There was nothing to see but the sun's glare, and it seemed to reach into things she wanted to hide. Hetty began again. "I know he's been good to you."

Morgan joined in the praise. "Yes, when Dad was drinking heavily, the commander took me under his wing. He guided me through the maze of college applications. He couldn't have been kinder."

Hetty gripped the headboard and looked at Morgan's shoulder. The message in his eyes was predictable. He loved hearing of her appreciation for others, and that's what he would expect.

"Well," she said, "it's hard to be disappointed in people . . . I mean to hear things that are not like you thought . . ." Hetty kept watching his shoulder.

He smiled. "There's nothing that could disappoint me about the commander. He's a hero to me."

The sun was going down. Hetty watched the last beam of fading light come through the window. It captured tiny flecks of lint. They floated, fell, and disappeared—like living things that could only exist because of the light.

"Where were we?" Morgan asked. "Did I interrupt you?"

Hetty directed her words toward Morgan's shoulder, and his shoulder listened to the whole experience. As she told of it, Hetty stiffened with the revulsion she had felt on that car ride. While hearing herself talk, she remembered her papa saying he had once been in a runaway car.

Hetty felt like her brakes had failed. She needed to drive off the road to find an escape.

Welcome relief came when Morgan cradled her in silence.

What could Morgan be thinking? Maybe there was nothing he could say to help anyway, but Hetty needed to hear *some* response. Anything would be better than waiting.

Then it came.

He asked, "Could you have misinterpreted his actions?"

She had not. Hetty relived the sleaziness of the ride in that car but said nothing. She had the sickening feeling Morgan didn't believe her.

"And what did your parents say?"

"I didn't tell them."

"Shouldn't you have told them right away?"

Hetty pulled away to look out the window again. The repugnant memory returned, and her stiffness with it.

"It was too hard to talk about. I couldn't have described my feelings at that age." His mistrust was unbearable. "You do believe me, don't you?"

His eyes flashed. "What kind of man do you think I am? Do you think so little of me?" He paused to catch himself. "Did anything else happen?"

"No."

"I'm sure my sister went to their house, but Melinda never had an experience like that. I would have known."

Hetty was not so sure. But she said nothing. She couldn't bear to hear another question and wanted to clamp her hands tight over her ears. Instead she examined her own reactions.

No matter what he might say, I've got to be strong. How can I expect Morgan to understand? The idea of being vulnerable is outside his experience.

"I'm sorry," he said. "Maybe I just don't *want* it to be true. And you know how imaginative you are."

Hetty lied to him. "I understand," she said. Her lie stopped his questions. But nothing stopped the tension. A spasm caused her neck to jerk, so she leaned against the window to hold her head still. Morgan gave her a stiff, unnatural hug. It was worse than nothing, but he probably meant well. Or was it evidence that he thought she was somehow unclean?

He seemed distant and moody. Soon a security officer returned to say Morgan's legal services had been requested, and they left together. When the door closed, Hetty remained alone, struggling to make sense of Morgan's response.

CHAPTER SIX

The Confession

Hetty dreaded Morgan's return. When the officer escorted him back to the room, she was still sitting where she had been earlier. Taking her hand, he kissed her cheek without the stiffness she had expected.

He sat. "Ben died today."

Hetty's shock was apparent. She stared at him, hoping it was some sort of joke.

Morgan continued. "According to the doctor's examination, he died from poisoning. Sophie says she poisoned him."

"No! Why would she do it?"

"To inherit his money."

"Well," said Hetty, "I don't believe her."

"Other passengers heard Ben talk about leaving her money. I think Sophie was more than a housekeeper. And Security is questioning Troy. There are rumors he's interested in her."

Hetty nodded. "Well, that's one thing I do believe."

"So do I. It seems some of the passengers saw Troy enter Ben's room to take him food. They think he could have poisoned Ben."

"What does Stewie think about all this?"

"Because of his age, they're handling him tactfully."

Hetty stood, then sat again. "Morgan, I don't see why Sophie would poison him to get money she was going to inherit anyway."

Morgan pondered that briefly and said, "You thought Ben had some hold over her. Maybe she'd had enough of being controlled."

Hetty had a new thought. "Stewie didn't like him, but he couldn't have done it. Could he?"

"I wonder."

Morgan stood and picked up the phone. "Maybe Security will let us both talk with Sophie. You'll be better than I was at getting the truth out of her."

The security officer said *no*.

Everyone who had sat at Ben's table would be under their watch pending arrival of the local police. Only at the conclusion of the investigation would they be allowed to disembark.

I Had to Do It

In the morning, Hetty saw a police boat anchored next to the *Queen Mary*.

Most of the passengers disembarked when they arrived in Southhampton, but the people who had spent the most time with Ben remained. The eight of them were being held for questioning in the library. Sophie sat alone, twisting her handkerchief. She looked pale and strained. Stewie sat on a stool swinging his legs.

Hetty and Morgan had been the last to arrive. If there was some explanation for their all being seated so far apart, Hetty had no idea what it was. The center of the carpet held everyone's attention. After inspecting that spot, Hetty saw no reason why it should. Leaving her seat next to Morgan, she crossed the room and placed a chair next to Sophie.

"I'm so sorry about Ben. Are you all right?"

Sophie nodded.

Hetty continued. "Whatever happened, it couldn't have been your fault."

Sophie's voice was a whisper. "Thank you."

"How long did you work for him?"

Sophie looked at the carpet. She didn't respond until tightening the twist in her handkerchief.

"Like I told the police, I . . . I poisoned him." Her eyes were wide and continued to stare at the carpeting. "I told Morgan the same thing."

Hetty put an arm around her. "How long had you and Ben been married?"

"Just since . . ."

Stewie stopped swinging his legs. "You *married* him?" He stared at his mother with his mouth open.

"Please, Stewie," she said. "Please . . . I didn't mean to keep it secret." As her hands shook, the handkerchief vibrated. Hetty remembered the wings of the fly.

Sophie began to cry but gulped the air and continued. "I was hoping you and Ben could make friends. We were going to tell you after that."

"But Mom," Stewie's voice squeaked, "I mean, how come?"

"Ben planned to pay for your college," she said. "*I* couldn't afford it."

"But he was a creep . . ."

When Sophie held up her hand, Stewie was quiet.

She said, "Ben was lonely and wanted to be a better man—and to make life better for Stewie and me. He kept saying he would put me in his will." Sophie looked frail and frightened, as if unable to stop talking. "But the only way I could be sure of getting his money was to marry him. Ben arranged for Captain Bonnard to marry us our first morning on the ship. He promised to keep it secret. If I didn't go along with it, there were . . . certain things he threatened to say about me. You can see why I had to do it. I didn't know till we were married, that Ben planned to send Stewie away."

Stewie looked at Troy, who appeared profoundly disappointed.

Hetty was stunned. How could she have been so mistaken about Sophie?

Taking the Blame

As the police inspector entered the library, all eyes turned to him. First, he thanked everyone for their cooperation.

Resting the clipboard against his belt, he explained their findings. "Ben must have thought he was drinking the ginger ale he ordered. His prescription says *do not take with alcohol.* But Mr. Kawada saw him take the wrong drink before he left to lie down. Apparently, he took his first pain pill just before resting.

"When Sophie entered, he was half asleep and probably forgot he'd already taken one. So, he asked her for another pill. Not long after that, Stewie looked in on him. The doctor says by then Ben would have been barely conscious—but still remembering his pain. Stewie gave him the pill he requested at about two o'clock. Soon after that, his nervous system became severely depressed. The doctor estimates the time of his death to be around six o'clock."

This description of the crime seemed to agitate Sophie, and she interrupted the inspector. "But officer, Stewie never went into Ben's room. I had other errands for him to do."

Stewie spoke up. "What do you mean, Mom? I remember the pill bottle. It said *Dolphin* on it."

The inspector corrected him. "Dolophine," he said. "A brand of methadone."

Sophie interrupted him. She was visibly shaken. "No, no! Stewie's confused. I'm the one. I gave Ben two pills," she said, "so I'm sure he died before Stewie went in." She blinked and looked around the room at all the surprised faces. "I mean if Stewie *had* gone in, Ben would have been dead already."

The inspector seemed just as surprised. "You're all free to go," he said. "Mr. Benutto's death was an unfortunate accident."

Stewie was confused. "Why did you make up stuff, Mom?"

Morgan took him aside and explained, "Your mother was very courageous. She cares more about you than about her own self."

Hetty went to Sophie. "The truth was bound to come out."

"What should I do now?" Sophie asked. She looked lost and helpless.

Morgan advised her to be cautious. "In case Ben may have made some borderline shady deals, take it slow with the inheritance. I know he planned to take you to his villa outside of Paris. If I were you, I'd put off going there. In fact, it could be wise not to inquire about it right away. Ben may owe money to some dangerous men. I'll do some fact-finding if you like."

"Yes . . . please . . . I'll admit I'm frightened. I don't know what I'll do after you leave."

Hetty and Morgan agreed to stay with Sophie until after the funeral and burial.

Stonehenge

The air was dank in the Southhampton port, and the fog was thick. Starting at seven that morning, Hetty heard the commotion of suitcases being shuffled in the hall. Though the other passengers disembarked early, the eight who had been held for the investigation were allowed a more leisurely departure.

The first to say goodbye was Joan. As for the others, some of their previously made plans would need to change.

Miko didn't want to lose sight of Hetty until her marriage fears could be solved. Sophie was depending on Hetty for moral support and on Morgan for legal advice. Stewie wanted to follow wherever Troy decided to go, but Troy was in a hurry to leave.

Hetty noticed Sophie and Troy never made eye contact. In fact, they couldn't be more conspicuous about avoiding each other.

Morgan picked up a newspaper and showed Hetty an article on the front page. "News travels fast," he said. It was just a few lines. The heading read, *Foul Play in "Ben" Benutto Death?*

He tucked it under his arm and asked, "Who wants to see Stonehenge?" It was a welcome opportunity to delay decisions, and Morgan arranged transportation for all of them.

At Stonehenge, the fog lifted to expose a blue sky. Hetty laid her jacket on the damp grass and leaned back against one of the great stones. They were far taller than she had expected; however, it was their age that inspired awe.

The peace of the moment appealed to Hetty more than the thought of exploring. She closed her eyes to let the sun warm her face and remained there listening to the birds. Had ancient people leaned against the same huge uprights five thousand years ago? Had they listened to the birds?

Thinking herself alone, she was startled to hear Sophie's voice. "I'm sorry if . . . if I'm interrupting anything," she said.

Hetty smiled and spread her jacket to offer more seating space. "Not at all."

After a long silence, Sophie opened the conversation. She spoke timidly. "You must think I'm horrible. I'm sure Stewie does."

Hetty shook her head. "If he doesn't realize you confessed for his sake, I'm sure Morgan will explain it to him."

"I know. What I really meant was . . . I meant about marrying Ben." A tear rolled down her cheek. "It was my first chance for a respectable life. Ben promised me security."

"Also," said Hetty, "I imagine you've been worried about Stewie's future."

"Yes. Stewie won't believe me, but I was growing fond of Ben."

"Of course, you were," said Hetty. "When you're trying to make someone happy, it's only natural that you'd learn to care about him. You were attentive to his needs. We all saw how you looked out for his comfort."

Sophie twisted her handkerchief. "Thank you for saying that." Putting her head back, she sighed. "Ben had me room with Stewie. And he wouldn't let me wear my wedding ring. He insisted on getting Stewie's approval first. But he did all the wrong things to earn it." She wiped her eyes. "I've seen how much Stewie admires Morgan and Troy. I wish Troy didn't have to leave. Even if he hates me, I'm sure he wouldn't take it out on Stewie."

"Hate wouldn't be the word," said Hetty. "When Troy thinks back over the week, he'll see you didn't show any special interest in him. You were a devoted wife, and you never led Troy to believe otherwise."

"But Hetty, I feel so foolish . . . I only knew Ben a few months! He's the first man who ever made me feel special."

Hoping to cheer Sophie, Hetty mentioned something her papa used to say. "A hundred years from now you'll no longer know it happened."

Hetty tried to smile as she spoke, but she couldn't. Pressing her back against the ancient stones, she thought of Morgan's response to the Slubbet event. That disturbing conversation continued to weigh on her, and she doubted if five thousand years would be enough to erase it from her memory.

Miko came from behind them and addressed Hetty. "If you don't mind, I think we should stay in the same hotel as you and Morgan. With you nearby, Father might see Kenzo through your eyes."

Until now, Hetty had hoped she could help Miko. But now she wondered if Morgan would be more sympathetic with Mr. Kawada's point of view.

After all, for ten years he accepted the idea of an arranged marriage with Katrinka.

When the men were ready to leave, Morgan helped Hetty and Sophie to their feet. The ground was wetter than they had thought, and Hetty's jacket was soaked all the way through. She wanted to hide. Her skirt was stained with mud.

Before they drove away, Morgan spread his newspaper on the seat under her. "I wish I'd brought a cloak to put in the mud for you," he laughed. "Like Sir Walter Raleigh."

They were not alone, but Morgan took her hand in his and whispered that he wished they were.

They would be in Paris soon. Maybe everything would be all right.

Paris

Hetty parted the lace curtains. "It's the perfect small hotel, Morgan! It's close to the Metro—close to everything! I can even see the Boulevard Saint-Germain from here."

"I'm glad you like it. This was Troy's suggestion. We can get the same room when we get back from the Riviera."

Hetty's eyes shone with excitement. "Really? We're going to the Riviera?"

"Not yet." Morgan wore a somber expression. "First, I'll have to leave you here while I take a quick trip. Troy knows I want to have you to myself. He offered to look out for Stewie and Sophie when I return, so we can go to the Riviera— for Stewie's sake. I told him about the newspaper article. We agreed Sophie mustn't leave the hotel. She may have reason to fear whatever thugs Ben owed money. Troy can take food to her, show Stewie around Paris, and translate for them both. Also, since the Kawadas want to see Paris, they'll stay here to meet Kenzo. You won't be alone."

Hetty cranked open the casement windows to let in the street sounds. "I'll miss you," she said. She hurt all over at the thought of his absence, but she decided not to tell him so. "When do you have to go?"

Morgan stood behind her. "Now," he said. His arms tightened around her waist.

Hetty would hold the memory of his warm breath behind her ear. Maybe it would give her strength. Where was he going, and how would he get there? She must be strong and let him go without asking. What scheme might Katrinka have in mind this time? She couldn't help wondering, because there was always something. How did Katrinka manage to get away with so much?

Hetty thought of when Morgan was kidnapped. It was Katrinka's foolish plan, and it went dangerously wrong. After the nightmare was over, she had people believing she was his rescuer. Did Morgan ever figure out the truth? Hetty did, but it would have seemed vindictive to say anything.

During that disaster, she and Katrinka promised to be friends. But did Katrinka ever intend to keep her promise?

Hetty held Morgan's arms in place and laid her cheek back against his. The smell of him made her giddy. A soft breeze ruffled the curtain. Closing her eyes, she felt herself flying with him high above the clouds, wrapped together in a white lace curtain.

Clean and pure. Above the world. Away from Katrinka.

What's the Point?

The white starched tablecloths, the crisp cheerfulness of the breakfast room—it was more charming than Hetty expected. A waiter, in his black and white uniform, greeted the party of six and directed them to a sunny table by the window.

Stewie was soon nibbling on a piece of bread. "Where did Morgan go?" he asked.

Hetty hoped Troy might answer, but he looked as if he didn't know either.

"I think on . . . on business," she said, "somewhere." There followed an awkward awareness that wives normally know such things.

"It figures," said Stewie. "Seems like he's always, you know, making arrangements."

The silence was uncomfortable. Hetty looked through the lace curtains. They were the same as those upstairs in their room.

Stewie glanced up at Troy. "Why can't you still paint my mom? You can do it *here* just as good as some old villa." Sophie put her hand on his arm as a signal to stop that line of questioning.

But Hetty was sure Stewie had more on his mind. She remembered the story of the boy with his thumb in the dike. It couldn't be easy to keep the sea from leaking through the hole. Stewie seemed content to look out the window for now, but soon the dike would spring another leak.

Stewie watched the passing pedestrians and sighed. "I mean what's the point of anything?" he said. "How come half the people are going left while all the other guys go right. Why can't everyone just stay where they are in the first place? Get it? I mean it would turn out the same." He folded his arms and set them in place with an emphatic jerk. "I mean, how stupid!"

Hetty felt like applauding Stewie's sentiment. In fact, if it could bring Morgan back, she would have.

Troy laughed. "What about that fellow out there? The one with the loaf of bread under his arm. It's called a baguette. Would you have him stay home and miss out on the best bread in the world? At the boulangerie, they start making it at four in the morning."

Stewie tore off another piece of his crust. "So, is that what this is?"

"Yes. They always have five slashes. If it's long and thin like a wand, it's a baguette.

According to legend they were shaped so a soldier could fit one end in his pocket."

"Cool!" He looked at Troy with admiration and spread butter on the crust. Suddenly he sat up straight as if considering an extremely weighty matter. "I've been thinking. Tell me man to man, do people you paint have to be . . . um, real beautiful? Like is that a profession thing?"

"No. I paint whatever people pay me to paint."

Stewie fingered what would have been his beard if he'd had one. "Oh." After considering a moment longer, Stewie tried another approach. "Do you ever get to paint people that are real beautiful just 'cause you feel like it?" His eyes were big and round, and he was waiting.

Troy's face turned red. "Yes, I do."

Sophie stared straight ahead as if willing herself far away.

"Cool!" said Stewie. "Then you can paint my mom. I mean, unless you don't think she's pretty enough."

Sophie flushed and gave Hetty a desperate glance.

There was a noticeable increase of fidgeting around the table.

Troy was speechless.

"I know!" Stewie continued. "Lace curtains would look real terrific in the picture." Energy ramped up his excitement. "I bet Ben's villa doesn't have lace curtains." Suddenly, he seemed to notice the silence and lowered his voice. "But if you don't think she's pretty enough, I've got some allowance saved up."

Sophie gripped Stewie's hand and opened her mouth to speak, but Troy was quick to answer. "It would be a pleasure." He put an arm around Stewie. "And it won't cost you a thing."

Miko smiled at Stewie. "I think there's a point to everything," she said, "No matter what. That is, if we make things happen. The point is to make our own decisions, whatever the consequences."

Stewie had taken matters into his own hands. Hetty guessed Miko wasn't the only one to admire his initiative.

Mr. Kawada offered a gentle rebuttal. "I think individual not so important. All people have obligation to society." He bowed slightly and smiled. "Sometime old Japanese way best!"

Perhaps Sophie was still recovering from the earlier conversation, but she was next in line to express her view of life. She said, "I've deliberately tried not to think about it too much one way or the other. Besides, we may envision some purpose, and life makes us change directions." Her expression softened as she looked at Stewie. "That's how we muddle through one day at a time."

Suddenly, Stewie decided there were lots of purposes in life. But he'd need to borrow a pencil. As soon as he could make up a list, he'd like to say a whole bunch of them.

He looked to Troy and got an approving nod.

"Meanwhile," said Troy, "I believe people are greatly affected by their surroundings. And that we should be the means of transmitting whatever is good and beautiful. If it's a way to make people happy, maybe we should consider it an obligation."

Sophie looked impressed and, for the first time in two days, looked directly at Troy.

Hetty noticed and felt inspired to propose a plan. "Sophie," she said, "would you consider staying with me? If we double up while Morgan's gone, he'll see how thrifty I can be. That is, if Troy and Stewie are all right with rooming together." She turned to address Troy. "My room has good natural light. And the same curtains. Do you think you could paint in there just as well?"

So, it was decided. There was enthusiasm all around. Sophie couldn't very well have invited Troy to her room to paint, but now as the resident chaperone, Hetty could do all the inviting. She was relieved that the plans Stewie set in motion could now take place.

All eyes remained on Hetty, and she laughed. "Oh, is it my turn to make sense of life?" She waited a minute to think, feeling it was impossible to explain her thoughts. She said, "It seems like . . . the more people I love, the richer I feel. I think love gives us strength—helps us control our destiny."

Hetty felt weak from the words she heard herself say. Perhaps because she knew it was a truth greater than she could fully understand.

Cheerful chatter continued around the table, but it didn't hold Hetty's attention. Her mind wandered:

I know what love is. It's Morgan. Always and forever Morgan.

Papa says love grows with the exercise of it. I know he's right. It never wears out from overuse.

Maybe that's why these new friends matter to me.

Before Phil died, he asked me to love Katrinka. How do I make myself trust her? Maybe love can't always include trust, but I hope she'll keep her promise, and we can be friends.

I need to be in charge of how I feel. Nobody else can make me have hateful thoughts—unless I let them. Not even Katrinka. I need to do my best, or it's like living a lie.

Wherever Morgan is, I'm not sure he believed me about Slubbet. Does he think I made it all up to pretend the commander found me desirable?

I mustn't disappoint him. Have I already? If things were really good between us, wouldn't he still be here? If they're touring factories here in Paris, why did he take a suitcase?

Hetty felt the purpose of life would be empty without Morgan.

Raging Maniacs

Morgan carried only one suitcase. An older woman walking in front of him was struggling with two heavy ones. By tucking his own bag under his arm, he managed all three of them with ease. The woman's grateful smile revealed long yellow teeth and twinkling eyes. After thanking him, she said to no one in particular, "What a kind and handsome young man!"

The seats were not wide enough for Morgan's broad shoulders. But if the passenger next to him objected to the tight squeeze, he kept it to himself. Maybe the man spoke only French.

The question Morgan often heard was, *Are you traveling for business or pleasure?* This time he would keep his head down. That way he could avoid explaining the purpose of the trip. Maybe the solution was to stare at the pages of a magazine he did not intend to read.

Morgan had a lot of thinking to do.

How am I going to react when I get there? It's hard to predict, even after such a long relationship. Maybe I won't have to sever it.

Maybe Hetty thinks I'm in Germany. But I don't feel guilty.

How could I be so incredibly lucky to have her trust me so completely? Or maybe she didn't want to sound possessive.

If she had asked me, I couldn't have lied to her. But I still think it was better to spare her talking about it. Besides, she might have asked me not to go through with it.

I would have come anyway.

We've discussed the importance of honesty in our relationship. When Hetty finds out about this how will she react?

At the airport, Morgan stepped into the men's room and straightened his tie in the mirror. He was seldom concerned about his appearance, but this time, he wanted to get it right.

Soon he found himself in a taxi, mindlessly giving directions. The ride was long and smoke-filled. The driver tried to start a conversation about obnoxious people. He said if you put perfectly normal people behind a steering wheel, without exception, they become raging maniacs.

He had facts and figures to prove it. His firsthand involvement with such folks seemed rather extensive. Morgan thought it best to agree with the man before his fury endangered their lives.

When they were almost there, Morgan's muscles tightened. "Just half a mile on the right," he said. He could sense a rise in his adrenalin and wondered if it could be from some degree of eagerness. He hoped the veins in his neck were not standing out.

He tried to calm his mind.

Self-control. That's what Hetty would expect of me. Self-control and forgiveness. I must keep that in mind.

After the taxi drove away, Morgan stood still and imagined Hetty's face. He could see her pale lashes and the softness of her eyes.

It was not quite dark, but someone turned on the porch light to welcome him. He could remember how light formed a halo in the softness of her hair. He would hold tight to the vision of Hetty's innocence and the honeysuckle scent of her sweet breath. That way he could remember why he came.

Morgan pressed the doorbell. Above the door, a row of polished brass letters reflected the setting sun. They formed the name *Slubbet*.

His eyes narrowed. In spite of his efforts, he felt his anger rise.

CHAPTER SEVEN

The Commander

The commander's wife led Morgan to the study, where he received a warm welcome. On the wall beyond the desk were photographs of famous people. The most conspicuous one was of President Eisenhower and Commander Slubbet standing together.

In the past, the commander had seemed larger than life. He appeared to have shrunk.

He gave Morgan a firm handshake and dismissed his wife.

"I understand congratulations are in order," he said.

"Yes, I'm on my honeymoon. My wife probably thinks I'm in Germany."

"Well, we don't have to tell our wives everything, do we?" Slubbet laughed knowingly. Morgan didn't think it was funny, so an awkward pause followed. "Well, that Katrinka would be a hard one to leave!"

"I didn't marry Katrinka."

"I see. I'm sorry my wife and I weren't able to attend your wedding. I'm sure it was beautiful. Your family does everything to perfection."

"I married Hetty Lawrence."

"I don't believe I know her." Slubbet's eyes darted quickly around the room. "But there have been so many girls . . . I mean my daughters have always brought so many friends to the house."

Had Slubbet's eyes always being so shifty?

"Hetty and your daughter Susie were friends," Morgan said, "when they were both fourteen. She was in your home. You might remember her. She was very tall for her age—and thin." Slubbet seemed to remember, but he turned to look out the window.

"No," he said. "I would have remembered." He faced Morgan again, with a smile pasted on his face. He squinted. "Like I told the governor, I intend for this appointment to make a difference in your political plans. You have a promising future, if you play your cards right." He tilted his chin high. Morgan saw it as challenging gesture. "I was willing to overlook your past," he continued. "Like the fact that your father was a drunkard."

Morgan's fingernails dug into the palms of his hands.

Slubbet's sly smirk was infuriating. Had his face always been so greasy? He spoke again in a smooth and appeasing voice.

"Oh, I don't mean that to sound harsh. Your dear parents simply drank too much, like many of us. That's why I offered you my guiding hand when you applied for college. I said to my dear wife, someone as promising as young Morgan Morganthal shouldn't have to navigate that alone. And I'll always support you, my friend. Of course, I expect the same from you. I'm sure you understand me. I doubt if you're proud of everything *you've* done." Slubbet paused. Was he waiting for some sort of confession?

When Morgan didn't flinch, Slubbet tried another tack. "Men of your caliber are needed in Washington. Of course, to get that kind of power, you'll need my help. You know that. We can make a difference together, you and me. I wonder why a rising star like you didn't marry that beautiful Katrinka Wallace. You would have made quite the couple!

"I've been watching you, Morganthal. It's unfortunate the newspapers take such an interest in everything you do." A low chuckle came from deep in his chest. "I'm just saying people can find out what they want if they just look hard enough. I know Katrinka Wallace would say just about anything to get attention."

Slubbet wore a large diamond ring on his pinky finger. He tapped it on the desk and waited for Morgan's reaction. Hearing none, he added in a low, breathy voice, "I'd like a reason to protect you."

Morgan was quickly forgetting why he should be grateful to Slubbet. Even the things he had recently told Hetty now slipped his mind. He knew anything he might say to thank the commander could be taken as acceptance of his sleazy threat.

"I'm fortunate," he said. "In spite of past differences, I have a father who has been an example to me of the finest ethical behavior. And absolute marital fidelity. As you know, we were distant for some years. But I didn't have to be close to him to recognize his good character."

Morgan struggled against the red heat of anger. "I see my wife and my parents as the best influence on my past and future life. I am mindful of all you've done for me—and the example of your years of kindness."

He waited for the tension in his jaw to subside and said, "But most of all I value honesty in my relationships. I do not accept help that comes at the wrong price."

Morgan's glare was unwavering until he turned and closed the door to leave Slubbet's sneering face behind. When it was over he took a Boeing 747 again—this time heading back to France. He felt heavy-hearted with disappointment in his former hero. And maybe in himself. On the flight, Morgan tried to recall the conversation.

I became a monster in my head. I wanted to smash him against the wall and twist his arm. I could have broken it and thrown him to the floor to make him say he was sorry. I wanted to hear him beg for mercy.

But I knew Hetty would want me to have a kinder attitude.

I would do anything to protect her, if only I could go back in time. How dare he frighten her like that!

Morgan's fist pounded the armrest. "I won't have it!" he said.

Thoughtless Bungling

Troy almost finished Sophie's portrait in the three days Morgan was gone. Hetty couldn't smell turpentine in the room anymore. Sophie had moved back into her old room, but Stewie was hoping to stay on with Troy.

Morgan was due to return any time now. The maid had pushed the two double beds together in preparation for his return—apparently, to create her version of a honeymoon suite.

Hetty watched for Morgan through the curtains.

When she saw him across the street on the sidewalk, her heart sank. He was pale. Like a sculpture of cold marble. In one hand was his suitcase, in the other a large bouquet of flowers. He paused at a wrought-iron gate to look up at the window. Why didn't he come quickly?

Confused, Hetty unlatched the door and waited.

At first, Morgan made a halting entry, then eagerly embraced her like a starving man rushing to a life-sustaining meal. "Will you ever forgive me?"

His movements were anxious, and the flowers were forgotten.

"Of course, Morgan." She struggled to hold back the tears. "And I understand."

He held her tight. "I don't deserve you."

She was frightened to think what might have happened. "Please . . . please don't say that!"

His fingertips were in her hair, feeling her face, the dimple in her chin. His lips brushed her cheek in a tender kiss. Then he waited, as if questioning the right to her lips.

His remorse was deep and sincere. "It won't happen again," he said.

Hetty tried to appear composed, but she wasn't sure how to respond, with all the questions swimming in her head.

"I know," she said, "sometimes things just . . . happen. But you've taught me the importance of moving on."

"I love you, Hetty, and I believe in you. I was almost here before I realized how I must have hurt you. When I saw you through the window, I was afraid to come up. After my thoughtless bungling, I don't trust my own words anymore. But I do want to show you I can be a better listener—if you'll give me another chance. Also," he said, "I need to explain the last three days. They won't count as a business expense. But first I need to shower and change. I reek of cigarettes after the plane trip."

"The plane? I thought she . . . weren't you here in Paris?"

The Riviera

From their small hotel, Hetty looked out at the sparkling bright blue sea. The lunch-hour crowd had begun to gather at the little café, a floor below. Hetty leaned over the balcony railing to watch the people of Nice going about their business or walking to the beach.

Morgan had already arranged for a boat to take them from Nice to a quiet island cove. In preparation for the afternoon, Hetty wore her bathing suit under a light cover-up. They would soon leave. But for the moment, Morgan was on the phone. Hetty could barely hear his end of the conversation.

Would there be a change of plans?

She went inside and sat next to him on the bed. He hung up the phone and explained he would be going to Germany and Czechoslovakia shortly. As his serious dark eyes turned toward her, his hair fell over his forehead. "But if we go to the cove and back," he said, "I can still make the train." He continued to regard the phone as the enemy. "I'm sorry so much of our honeymoon has to be a business trip."

"Of course it does," she said. "I understand." Hetty would try to be thankful for whatever time they could spend together.

Suddenly she had no interest in the beach. The time it would take to talk to people about details, to go there and back, to walk through the lobby—it would all be a loss of time she would resent. Hetty couldn't bear the thought of sharing Morgan today.

She wanted to see his lips part in a smile for her alone. She ran her fingers along his arm, smoothing the hairs, and put her hand in his.

A smile appeared as she had hoped, and he said, "Are you thinking what I'm thinking?"

Hetty laughed in agreement, and Morgan called to cancel the boat. Without words, they expressed gratitude for this gift of time and stayed in to make joyful use of it.

After a while they were drawn to the balcony by the fresh air. The hotel manager had sent them a basket of fruit and cheese, which they carried out with them.

A profusion of bright bougainvillea vines provided privacy. Morgan admired the explosion of color and looked more closely.

"They're not flowers at all," he said. "They're leaves—thin and papery like tissue paper. The little white thing in the middle must be the blossom."

Hetty couldn't bear the thought of sharing him today.

Hetty liked having a reason to touch his hand, so she felt the same white blossom. She said, "The first European to see bougainvillea was a woman."

He glanced at her with admiration. "How did you know that?"

"From Father. He likes mentioning things like that. There aren't many women in his botany classes, and he lets them know they're just as capable as the men." Hoping her comment hadn't sounded too assertive, Hetty chose not to look at Morgan. She continued. "The French navigator Bougainville sailed around the world, in the 1700s. He took along two professional botanists. One of them was Jeanne Baré. She had to go disguised as a man, because women weren't allowed on the ships."

"How did she get away with it?"

"She was traveling with another botanist. Everyone thought she was his valet."

"Surely, *he* knew her secret."

"Yes, but she was his . . . his . . . lover."

Hetty wasn't sure why she blushed at the word—or why she had even mentioned it. Oddly enough, the very fact that she found it awkward was what was most embarrassing about it.

Morgan redirected his attention to the bougainvillea. Clearly it was to put her at ease, and she loved him for it.

"If we planted it back home at the cottage," he asked, "would it live? Maybe it needs a gentle climate."

Hetty felt herself dissolving in his kindness—the gentle climate he provided for her insecurities. If this balcony should forever seem special, he would be the reason. Many places would hold the same importance in her memories—all of them were marked by the freedom to show him her most tender sentiments.

The occasional lazy breeze was not enough to relieve the increasing warmth of the day, and Morgan helped her off with her cover-up. Then he pulled two tufted lounge chairs together, and they both stretched out in the shade.

A peculiar thought occurred to Hetty. They had gone to many amazing places. But why had they spent money to go on a honeymoon, when the perfect home was waiting for them?

She realized one reason might be to discover how little difference the location made. She would love Morgan the same whether at the cottage, in an airplane, or on the high seas. Of course, the cottage had been the scene of many joyous memories, and it would be again. Even without children.

Hetty thought of the childless couples she knew. Some centered their lives around their pets. Maybe that would be worth discussing. She sighed.

"Morgan, would you ever want a dog?"

"What kind?" he asked.

"I don't know . . . maybe a border collie? It would be extremely intelligent and very attentive. Though I'm not sure they're especially disease resistant."

"It would have to be death resistant."

She laughed. "You could take it for walks, and it would be all excited to play with you when you get home."

Morgan stretched, placed his hands behind his head, and grinned. "I was counting on you, for that."

"But truthfully," he added, "I don't want to get attached to something that would die."

He reached toward her, then suddenly appeared to think better of it. Hetty wondered if he realized his mention of death might appear to be about her heart. Probably not—it would be an issue only if she got pregnant.

"Hetty . . . I've never needed to account for money I spend, but I need to tell you about my last trip. It was something I had to do."

She knew it wasn't just about the money, but she wanted to pretend it was. She asked, "Will the adjustment be hard for you? I mean having to watch your spending."

"Probably not. My parents' lifestyle was never my choice. I don't need a lot of 'stuff and things.' Your family has always been a model for me."

He stood. For a moment he looked down at her earnestly. His eyes were the intense color of the blue heavens. Hetty tried to memorize his silhouette against the white clouds. She held her breath, unable to swallow.

He said, "We shouldn't love anything that can't love us back. My wants are few."

Hetty thrilled at the knowledge that she was his want.

He touched her hand. "We have some talking to do," he said.

"I know."

But anything he might say about Katrinka was sure to disturb the perfection of the moment, so she didn't encourage him to continue.

The time came for Morgan to pack, and he suggested that she stay and rest. "You look so comfortable," he added. "I'll change fast." He pulled off his tee shirt, and Hetty noticed how much his scars stood out in the heat.

She thought of four years earlier when Morgan had been caring for one of the circus elephants. It had stepped on him, crushing his hips, legs, and pelvis. He had been near death. To be near him, Hetty had stayed in the hospital as a stowaway. It was then she knew home was with Morgan, wherever he was.

While remembering all this, Hetty dozed off. Morgan returned to give her a goodbye kiss. Perhaps in a dream . . . slow and sweet, it lingered on her lips, but not long enough.

Three o'clock came and went. All protective shade had long since disappeared, and the burning rays of the afternoon sun beat down on Hetty's fair skin.

Even the clatter of dishes from the café below failed to wake her.

Vive La France!

In Germany, Morgan haggled over the Ferris wheel for two days before rejecting the terms of the contract. He walked away rather than falling for their now-or-never threat. He knew wisdom often required being slow and deliberate. Perhaps he would reconsider the deal after his trip to Czechoslovakia. But for now, he would take his time.

But that was the last thing on his mind right now. Morgan could think only of Hetty. He pictured the way she tilted her head to listen, the light in her eyes, her soft pink cheeks.

Suddenly, something in him snapped. How could they be under the same sun yet so far apart? With sudden resolve, Morgan stood and clapped his hands.

It would be complicated, but he worked fast. With the help of strangers, he rearranged his trip. Instead of going straight to Czechoslovakia, he would take a detour to see Hetty in Nice. It would be only half a day, but it was worth it. Morgan flushed with excitement at the thought. The pulse in his throat became so rapid, he had to loosen his tie. Hetty would be surprised to see him.

He was on his way when suddenly a sickening thought occurred to him: what if she should be at the beach? He could never find her there. Or shopping. She wasn't expecting him before the end of the week, so she could be anywhere— even ready to step out from the hotel.

He'd better call her right away!

At the train station, Morgan entered a phone booth. But the instructions were in French. While he struggled to decipher them, the man next in line tapped on the glass impatiently.

Morgan opened the door to apologize for the delay. His ninth-grade French was inadequate; however, the man understood his frantic pantomime. Furthermore, the word *honeymoon* made his face light up with enthusiasm. Squeezing into the booth with Morgan, he helped him call the hotel. As they waited for the switchboard operator, several passers-by collected around them with helpful suggestions.

Honeymoon seemed to be the magic word for attracting attention. Apparently, in France the separation of honeymoon couples was considered a national emergency. Morgan would not have been surprised to see a police escort appear.

At last the operator reported Hetty was in her room. In fact, someone from the front desk would stand guard to make sure she didn't leave.

A general cheer rose from the well-wishers. In the commotion, Morgan completely forgot how to say *thank you* in French. As the group rushed him to the train, all he could think of was *"Vive la France!"*

Upon detraining in Nice, Morgan was not at all slow and deliberate in his quest for a taxi. Nor did he ask the driver to take his time. He laughed with anticipation. Soon he would lift Hetty in his arms and swing her around the room.

Half a Day

Morgan turned the brass key in the lock. He rapped lightly on the door before opening it a crack.

Hetty said, *"S'il vous plait laissez-le devant la porte!"*

Whatever it meant, Morgan could tell she was alarmed.

The room was a little dim. "Are you all right?" he asked. "Morgan?"

She would have answered his question, unless something was wrong. When his eyes were accustomed to the subdued light, Morgan saw what it was. Everything he could see of her was sunburned. She was spread across the bed with only a corner of the sheet covering where her swimsuit had been. She watched him with red, puffy eyes.

"I can't believe you've come!" she cried.

"You should see a doctor, if you haven't already."

"No, it hurts too much to get dressed."

Morgan pulled a chair up to the bed. "What can I do?"

"You can be here like this." She tried to smile, but her lips were cracked and swollen.

Two glasses next to the bed were empty. He returned with cold water and supported her head while she drank. It spilled and dribbled down her neck, but she claimed it felt good.

"I'm supposed to leave for Prague in a few hours," he said, "but maybe I should stay." He stroked her hair. The sun had bleached the little wisps around her temples.

"I'll be fine, now. Really. Tell me about Germany."

"Could we talk about something else?" he said. "Our time is so short."

Her palms were against the sheet, and he slipped his hand under hers.

She pressed it with her fingers and said, "A lot happened after you left Paris. Kenzo came from Tokyo to meet Miko. You'd be surprised how well that's going. And Troy started the portrait of Sophie. I think they're happy for an excuse to be together. He's stalling to make it take longer. I'm sure of it! He probably wanted us to leave Paris, so he could take care of Sophie and Stewie himself."

Morgan needed to tell Hetty about his trip to see the commander. He wondered why she seemed so opposed to hearing about it. This time, he launched into the explanation before she could forestall it.

"I went to see Slubbet last week," he said. "I didn't tell you beforehand. I didn't expect it to fix anything, but I had to do it. I spent the whole flight planning what to say. When I got there nothing went as I intended."

Hearing no reaction, he took a deep breath and continued. "When you told me about him, I know you didn't think I believed you. I wanted to go back to the past and protect you. Of course, I couldn't, and that made me feel somehow responsible. That helpless feeling made me wake up and realize the position he put *you* in—how much more helpless you must have felt. You were completely powerless and vulnerable."

Hetty listened without comment.

"And then I made matters worse with my clumsy reactions. You were generous to forgive me," he said. "Slubbet was an influential man, and I've been thinking . . . if anything like that happened to my sister, maybe she wouldn't have dared tell me. Melinda might have assumed I would believe his word over hers. The commander probably counted on that." Morgan waited briefly, then began again. "If it was too hard to tell your parents at the time it happened, it would have been even more difficult later. You'd wonder if they might feel guilt over letting you down—or why you hadn't trusted them to believe you in the first place. The damage goes on and on."

Hetty turned her eyes to Morgan. "Maybe we can make sure it doesn't."

"But Hetty. . . I should have seen him for what he was. I despised the way he made me feel. I had a real hatred for him, till I got control of myself."

"Please don't, Morgan. If we . . . if we feel like that about him, he wins. When I was fourteen," she said, "I couldn't bear to have you associate me with such an incident. And now, I feel even more that way."

Morgan was wishing he could make it all go away for her sake. Something had to be done, but resigning from the committee wouldn't accomplish anything.

All he could do now was try to make her comfortable. She felt better when he fanned her with the room service menu. The blue hairbrush was in her purse. She asked if he would use it to pull her hair back from her face. This was a new delight for Morgan. First, he rubbed her head, letting her silky curls fall through his fingers. Then he gathered her soft hair up over the pillow like a cloud.

Holding it in place with the other hand, he asked, "What do I do now?" He hadn't thought to be prepared with some sort of fastener. Or maybe he had but just wanted an excuse to repeat the process, which he did. This time he secured it with the sash of her robe, which he tied in a cockeyed bow.

"Thank you," she said. "That was wonderful, and I feel tidier."

He kissed the crown of her head and again suggested looking for a doctor. She promised to do so if she felt no better tomorrow.

Someone knocked. It was room service leaving a tray of food at the door.

"When you came," Hetty said, "That's who I was expecting." She couldn't eat anything, but Morgan helped her drink the juice with a straw. "I'm so sorry, Morgan. I don't mean to be so completely untouchable."

He smiled. "I'm just glad your teeth didn't burn."

"So am I . . . but I apologize about being so . . . so out of commission."

He put his hand under hers again and said, "I would have come anyway."

Morgan thought back to when Blossom had crushed him. His injuries were critical, but Hetty helped him keep a sense of humor. No one knew what parts of his body might be permanently disabled. He remembered a short poem she made up: *When trampling on organs, Why Morgan's?*

Hetty went away to college before he had recovered. They agreed on a rule to write each other only once a month, but Hetty found a way around it: she claimed a copy of her journal entry wouldn't *really* count as a letter. One page in particular, from her diary, gave him great comfort. He remembered it word for word:

The condition of Morgan's body has absolutely no bearing on whether I want to marry him. I'm not sure he believes me. He's afraid I don't know what I'm saying, but I do. I guess I'll need to propose to him again, if he is to believe me.

Morgan fanned Hetty again and watched her relax.

He must leave soon for Prague. Morgan would join the delegation going to Czechoslovakia at the invitation of the

Soviet ambassador. In the three years since 1957, Khrushchev had been promoting cultural exchanges. This would be a rare opportunity to go behind the Iron Curtain and see the influence of the famous Cirkus Kludsky.

Still, if Hetty needed him he would cut short his stay.

Morgan looked down at Hetty's hot red skin and wondered how severe the sun's damage might be. He hoped it would pass with time.

But Morgan considered damage of another sort. Where others might see the Slubbet incident as trivial, he now had a deeper understanding. He feared the effects of it could go on and on. Would she forever feel powerless and insecure? It might permanently affect her self-confidence.

And did she still worry about what she should have done differently? Feelings of guilt might damage her sense of worth. If so, Morgan feared his thoughtless questions had made the problem worse. He vowed to be part of the solution from now on.

When everything was in order, he laid his cheek against the softness of her hair and said a lengthy goodbye.

Morgan wanted nothing more than to stay and take care of her. It pained him to close the door and walk away. He felt fiercely protective. No one was going to push her around. She was so vulnerable . . . he must always shelter her from harm.

Luckily, she hadn't spoken of law school recently. If necessary, he would keep her from going, for her own good.

CHAPTER EIGHT

Dear Parents

Two days after Morgan left, Hetty felt a lot better. The swelling in her face was down. Either the passage of time had taken care of it, or it was the aspirin Morgan left for her on the bedside table.

None of her clothes were loose enough to wear with comfort, so she wasn't able to leave the room yet. Maybe she would tomorrow. But for now, she could manage with room service.

Hetty planned to write to her parents this morning. She took some stationery out to the shade of the balcony. Maybe the sea breeze would relieve the heat of her sunburn.

She could picture life back home. It would be nighttime now, and all would be quiet—although sometimes a mockingbird might surprise them with a song on summer nights. Before long, she and Morgan would be there. Maybe they would be sound asleep in the cottage, and then at midnight the mockingbird would start singing for the sheer joy of it. They would throw open the windows, then run out to the front porch in their pajamas. The moonlight would be sifting through the trees. They would lean their backs together and listen to the performance.

Hetty wiped her pen. Her more personal feelings were beyond explaining, but she sat at the small round table and wrote from her heart.

We're in the south of France, where I fell asleep in the sun, and I have a miserable sunburn. Morgan came all the way back from Germany to see me . . . for just half a day. Those few hours with him were a dream come true.

. . . I love knowing he is really mine. I'm indescribably happy!

Hetty thought about Morgan's unexpected visit. The floppy hairdo he devised made her laugh. She wanted to preserve it as long as possible, as a reminder of their half day together.

Morgan seemed to know her mind better than she did. She was touched that he had taken the time to think it through.

He was going to agree to her school plans, she could tell.

Hopes Derailed

Hetty took one last lingering look at the brilliant blue of the Mediterranean Sea. She and Morgan were sorry to leave their hotel, but the time had come to thank the manager and settle their bill. At the Nice-Ville train station they boarded the Mistral Rapide on their way to Paris. It moved rapidly along the coast for a time before moving inland.

Hetty sighed. "It would have been nice to stay longer."

Morgan took an appointment book from his breast pocket. "Yes, Nice was nice. Now, if they'd just turn down the sun."

Hetty watched Morgan's reflection in the window. A man that handsome turned heads. Hetty knew she and her husband appeared mismatched, but that was nobody's business.

They would be a better match if they had the law in common. But how could she bring up the subject? She would have to ease into it, not too directly. This train trip to Paris would be long enough that she would find a way.

"About the circus," she said. "I'm sorry you were disappointed. Did you meet any of the Kludsky family members?"

"We probably saw some, because the original founder had twenty-one sons. A lot of them were performers and animal trainers. We were treated very well, but we couldn't wander without a guide watching us every minute. And the performers couldn't talk freely. It was all about demonstrating the glory of their socialist system. Not so much about individual people. At one time, Cirkus Kludsky had 700 animals and 200 vehicles. It's hard to imagine an operation that huge. Now the circus has been nationalized, and the Soviet control feels oppressive. The government has taken over the puppet theater as well."

"How sad," said Hetty. "When they see how recently Japan was considered our enemy, shouldn't that give them hope for some kind of reconciliation?"

"It's hard to know. I doubt if Czechoslovakians dare talk about things like that." He put his appointment book away and said, "I know Miko will be glad to see you. Everywhere you go, you make a difference."

Maybe what he meant was *it doesn't take a law degree to improve the world*. Hetty wasn't sure she should mention her plans yet.

"Thank you," she said, "but tell me if it ever seems like meddling."

"It never does—you've got such good instincts. I had no relationship with my father until you came along. And to think my parents lived separate lives for twenty years. Ignoring each other in the same house."

"They already cared for each other," said Hetty. "They just didn't know it."

Morgan laughed. "Well, they do now. Their first honeymoon was a disaster, but they're certainly making up for lost time. You helped them see the best in each other."

"It wasn't hard to see. I love both your parents, and I admire them. There's so much of your father in you."

"Really, Hetty—I know it took courage to break the ice between them. It was a bold move."

Hetty wondered why Morgan was purposely showing all this confidence in her. Could he be picturing her name on the door next to his? Lawrence, Morganthal & Morganthal. She would wait and see.

"And when Ben died," he said, "you got Sophie to open up. You're amazing."

They rode in silence a while, and Hetty planned out the best approach.

I could tell him how often I see the need to be trained in the law. That's how I imagine us progressing together. I don't feel like I have much else to offer. But I can't say that when he's been trying to build my confidence. I don't need to mention the danger of having children . . . or not being permitted to adopt, with my heart condition.

"Morgan, I've been worried about how to tell you . . . there's something you should know. I want you to be happy for me," she said. "I've been accepted to law school."

"Of course you have." Morgan looked out the window.

"I want to go."

Didn't he hear that last part? He was still looking out the window.

He looked serious and thoughtful when he spoke. "Don't ever worry about telling me things. We can't keep secrets from each other."

Secrets. Maybe I should tell him I saw the telegram from Katrinka. No, it's a secret he should tell me first. If he's not talking, neither am I.

"And Hetty, I know you worry about money. You don't need to. I'll always provide for you. And it will give me more pleasure than you know."

While You Were Away

When they returned to their Paris hotel, Hetty looked at her peeling skin in the mirror.

Morgan stood behind her. "It's the post-Riviera look," he said. "You'll start a new trend." Pulling back her hair, he kissed the side of her neck.

Hetty was still trying to forgive the way he had changed the subject on the train. But that was an entirely different matter; she didn't want him to stop nibbling on her neck, and she tilted her head to make it known.

It's good to be back in Paris," she said. "Let's not go anywhere for a while."

Morgan lifted his head and their eyes met in the mirror. "I'm afraid I've made an appointment for tomorrow."

Somehow, Hetty knew this had to do with the Katrinka's telegram. They locked eyes, but he wasn't going to tell her more than that.

"And I'll need you to come with me," he said.

They heard something at the door. Hetty opened it to find Sophie trying to push a note through the crack and invited her in.

"Oh! I didn't know if you were back." Sophie sat on the chair Hetty indicated. "So much has happened while you were gone. Mostly I wondered if Morgan learned anything about Ben. You know . . . from his commander friend."

Morgan heard and joined in the conversation. "I thought of somebody better to do the investigating. I've called Jack Anderson."

"What! The newspaper columnist?

"Yes. He has connections and knows how to find the facts. He doesn't care how unpopular the truth makes him."

"Thank you, Morgan. That's a complication I hope to put behind me."

When Hetty asked if Troy had finished the portrait yet, Sophie smiled and said *no*. Maybe she could tell he was stalling.

Sophie changed the subject. "Troy hasn't heard back from his brother yet. He and Stewie are at the market now," she said. "Every day, Troy goes out for bread and cheese and fruit, and when he gets back, we eat together in the lobby. I feel safe the way he's been watching over me. He'll show us around Paris. That is, if you find out it wouldn't be dangerous."

The Banana Seed Wedding Gift

Next morning, Hetty could tell Morgan was happy about the appointment. He was attempting to hide it, but he was flushed with excitement. He had a driver pick them up from the hotel at dawn.

The happier Morgan seemed, the more Hetty dreaded seeing Katrinka. He squeezed her hand, and she failed to respond. Maybe he thought she would be happy to see someone from home. How could he be so insensitive as to think Katrinka would be that person?

Hetty knew she should attempt a little optimism. She tried to recall what Katrinka has said in their most recent conversation. She was somewhat apologetic about her conniving and asked, *Are you my friend, Hetty? Do you think it will always be that way?* Hetty had answered, *Yes, we'll always be friends.*

They would be thoroughly connected, and forgiveness would be more important than ever before.

There was another way to look at things: Katrinka's father, Phil Wallace, was dead now. He had been a friend, inspiration, and father figure to Morgan. Hetty knew better than to sever a tie like that. Until Katrinka was nine years old, she considered Morgan her best friend. He was three years younger than Katrinka, but their fathers had made big plans for them. Permanent plans.

Maybe Morgan saw no reason to give her up now.

Hetty hardly noticed the lush green countryside as they whizzed by. She stared at the side of the road and remained lost in thought. At a crossroad, the driver honked at a reckless pedestrian and muttered, *"Quel imbécile!"* Aside from that, they sat in silence throughout the ride.

When at last the car stopped at their destination, Morgan said, "Here we are."

Hetty was slightly irritated with such a useless statement of fact. Couldn't that be said at any time or place? *Here we are at the principal's office. Here we are stuck in the mud. Here we are in the operating room.*

Then she saw it. Hetty gasped at the wondrous sight. How could she have failed to notice right away?

"Morgan! You mean . . . you mean *this* was the appointment?"

There was no Katrinka after all.

Spreading before them was a magnificent hot air balloon. Its red, white and blue stripes gleamed against the emerald green field. The morning sun hovered above the horizon—a great ball illuminating the sight.

Joy and humiliation combined to confuse Hetty's thinking. Morgan walked to her side of the car while she recovered her composure. When he opened the door, she embraced him—both to thank him and to somehow compensate for her misguided attitude.

A gentleman working among the crew hurried to greet them. "Ah, Morgan!"

Shaking his hand warmly, Morgan said, "Hetty, this is Kat Wallace."

What followed were pieces of a dream. Kat was Phil's brother—Katrinka's uncle. He introduced the crew and explained the procedure.

"The setup and inflation will take about half an hour," he said. "Then you'll see us flapping it, to get air in through this opening at the bottom—what we call the mouth. We need to fill up the envelope with enough air that our Cremation

Charlie can stand up inside." Kat laughed. He saw that would require an explanation. "The part that holds the hot air is called the envelope," he said. "Before we can inflate it, someone has to stand inside and hold it up, so the flames don't burn anything critical. Maurice—in the green shirt over there—he's our Cremation Charlie today." He nodded as Maurice went through the mouth. "We just hope he doesn't singe his eyebrows."

Another man held a line attached to the crown, to help steady the balloon. Hetty listened to the hissing of the tank and watched the flames. When the envelope reached about eight stories high, it swayed before them, straining against its tethers like an eager racehorse. The chase crew had their vehicles prepared. They would follow the course of the balloon and retrieve it wherever it might land.

Kat and two other men preceded Hetty and Morgan into the gondola.

"You'll hear the word *montgolfier*," said Kat, "that's French for hot air balloon. The Montgolfier brothers are famous here. They invented the balloon used for the first manned flight in the 1700s—right here in Paris. My brother Phil got me into this. He didn't want be the only one having fun."

Morgan laughed. "Maybe that's why he got me started gliding."

Kat opened the blast valve to send up more heat. "You can count on it," he said.

Rising slowly, they cleared the treetops. A soft breeze carried them gently over fields and meadows. The sky was a clear and perfect blue, and yet Hetty couldn't feel the quiet peace she knew was there. She had a lump in her throat. Everything was colored with shame and sadness of her own making. The landscape was clouded with gloom, and she tried to understand why.

I've been suspicious and ungrateful. There's no excuse for my moods. No one could be more fortunate. This was the secret

Morgan was keeping, all along. Did he sense my irritation and distrust? I mustn't let the wrong frame of mind damage our relationship.

If I'm going to be the right kind of wife, I need to grow up.

This would be a once-in-a-lifetime experience. She would try her best to enjoy it. Years from now, what if Morgan should ask her about this day? Would she struggle to remember?

She put her arm through his. His eagerness to please her—that would be her lasting memory. The gondola was constructed of wicker, and it made a quiet creaking sound. The song "Rock-a-Bye Baby" came to Hetty's mind, but she didn't say so.

"It's like a dream, Morgan!"

She could tell he was pleased.

Kat pointed out the chase team on the ground and said, "About the weather, it wasn't just pure luck. After we first set the date, Morgan and I had to keep changing it." Kat tugged briefly on a rope and asked, "You know how I got my name? Phil was four years old when I was born. He was so disappointed when I wasn't a dwarf like him, that our parents let him pick my name. He liked the Katzenjammer Kids in the funny papers, but they talked him into Kat as a compromise."

Hetty assumed Kat had in turn inspired his niece's name. "Did Phil name Katrinka after you?" she asked. Maybe that was enough to show she was comfortable mentioning her name. She hoped that was the end of that.

"Yes, and she's the same age as my daughter Libby."

Hetty remembered Katrinka had asked her cousin Libby to be a bridesmaid, and suddenly she resented both of them. Clutching the rim of the basket, she looked over the side.

Hetty knew she had to change her attitude.

Her mother once told of an experience she had as a child. Bananas were a rare treat, and she coveted the one Santa Claus put in her brother's stocking. At first, she whined and moped around. Then, when no one was looking, she stole it and hid behind the barn door.

Peeling it open, she made a tragic discovery: every bite revealed tiny black dots down the middle. Thinking it must be either rotten or infested with insects, she spat out each mouthful one by one and covered them all with straw. Hetty tried to work it out in her mind.

It was years before mother learned those had been the seeds. She decided she didn't deserve to enjoy the banana because of what she had done. And maybe the misunderstanding was punishment for her guilt.

It's the same with me. I've let the thought of that telegram from Kat ruin everything. It seemed like a rotten banana, but it was all in my mind—a misunderstanding.

All too soon, Kat released the drop line from the gondola. A member of the chase crew was there and grabbed it, guiding the basket to a safe landing. There was a general celebration with expressions of gratitude for the successful venture.

Kat winked at Hetty. "Phil had good things to say about you. And he would do anything for Morgan. Please think of this as a wedding gift."

Is It That Obvious?

It had been a full day. Back in the Paris hotel, Hetty tried to remember details about that morning. Such a spectacular event as a balloon ride should have put her in a joyous state of mind, but no such thing happened. She held her own attitudes responsible. In the past, her most vivid memories of flying with Morgan had nothing to do with reality but were rooted in her thoughts and dreams.

These regrets were on Hetty's mind when she heard a scuffle in the hall. Then came a heavy thud followed by a man's groan. When she opened her door, there was Troy lying face down on the carpet.

Sophie must have heard the same sound. She was running toward him. "No, no! Oh, Troy . . . I've done this to you! I'm sure they were coming for *me*," she sobbed. With her cheek against his back, Sophie embraced him. "Please forgive me!" Tears filled her eyes, and she used her handkerchief to wipe the blood from his face.

She stroked his hand. "Hetty, how should we get help?"

This tender scene had another witness. A man coming from the other end of the hall had seen everything. Rushing toward them, he dropped a bag full of bread, and cheese, and fruit.

"L. B.!" he cried.

It was Troy. Sophie looked up in surprise. When she did, Troy knelt down next to her and and covered her hand with his. "It's my brother," he whispered.

Sophie was speechless. The two men looked identical.

L. B. stirred and soon turned over on his back. "I'm sorry, O. B.," he said. "I fell against your door. I must have blacked out."

Hetty heard Sophie stammer something unintelligible, and she seemed unsure where to look. But she stood quickly to distance herself from the awkwardness. "I . . . didn't know. I mean how can I help?" Her emotional display of affection was unmistakable, but what was the full meaning of it?

L. B. seemed to feel better. "Sorry to be so . . . horizontal in front of the ladies," he said. "I must have been too excited to see Troy."

He remained stretched out on the hall carpet.

Though Sophie was quiet, she seemed to be taking it all in.

"Did he call you O. B.?" Hetty asked.

"It's for Older Brother," said Troy. "I'm ten minutes older."

Sophie moved away from Troy. "I'm glad he's all right," she said. She looked embarrassed and escaped to her room.

"Then L. B. is what," asked Hetty, "Little Brother?"

Troy nodded. He invited L. B. to lie down in his room, leaving only Hetty in the hall. She gathered the scattered apples and gouda cheese Troy had dropped.

When Troy remembered the string bag, he returned to pick things up.

"Hetty," he said, "please forgive me if this sounds too personal, but I'm guessing you understand the complications of marrying someone with a lot of money."

"Not really," she said. "Here's something you don't know: Morgan could have had money, but he doesn't. He made a choice against his father's wishes, so he's on his own."

"Oh. They've had a falling out?"

"No, not at all. As for my thoughts on the subject, I suppose we should have discussed money matters before marriage. Maybe the most important thing is having the same attitude about it." Hetty knew Troy, as an artist of modest means, was worried about Sophie with her inherited wealth. She said, "I'm guessing you've thought about this question yourself."

"Is it that obvious?" he laughed.

"Maybe so," said Hetty, "but with Sophie being so recently widowed, such a discussion between you seems unlikely."

"I know. But the way she comforted my brother—it does give me hope."

Hetty agreed and said, "Your kindness to Stewie must be a comfort to her through this whole mess."

Troy's expression brightened. "I'm sure Sophie would be more comfortable if you come eat with us. You can see why. You and Morgan could get her and Stewie to come along with you. I have enough chairs in my room, and I'll invite Mr. Kawada and Miko."

"Good idea," she said. "When Morgan returns from buying a toothbrush, we'll knock on Sophie's door."

Thank You, Katrinka

Hetty was expecting Morgan's return, when someone pounded frantically on the door. *"Monsieur! Madame! Le téléphone . . . en bas!"*

Who could be calling? Hetty didn't wait for the elevator but ran quickly down the stairs to the lobby. The receiver of the heavy black phone dangled off the end of the front desk. On one end, the muffled voice of the operator was speaking French to another who was too distant to hear.

The young man who had led her downstairs stayed at a tactful distance. Aside from that, the lobby was empty.

"I'm calling Mr. Morganthall!" said a frustrated woman. "Tell him it's Katrinka! Can you hear me?" she screamed.

"This is Hetty. Morgan's gone out."

"On your honeymoon?" She laughed. "You've got to be kidding! Well, then you'll have to give Morgan the message. Commander Slubbet asked me to go see him. He didn't say what for. To tell the truth I was real flattered at first, and he sure sounded charming. I figured maybe he wanted me to do something public, you know, like posing for pictures. I was ready to help him with fundraising. He asked me all sorts of questions about Morgan, and I told him, you know, just stuff. Harmless things. I just thought he was being sort of nice and friendly."

The phone went dead for a while. The young man clicked it a few times and handed it back to Hetty in working order.

"Hetty honey, are you there?" Katrinka began again. "The commander said he wondered what was behind our broken engagement. He was sure Morgan was quite the ladies' man. Then he said something real fishy. He said Morgan threatened him and made accusations. That's when I knew for sure he was a phony. He started flattering me, and when he tried acting forward, I gave him a piece of my mind. I slammed the door on him and walked out.

"I thought I'd better warn Morgan. But you'll have to tell him, now that I got you by mistake."

It's Going to Be Wonderful

Hetty felt guilty about the negative thoughts she'd had earlier. Katrinka had stood up to the commander, and she should be grateful. When Morgan returned with a toothbrush, Hetty told him about the phone call.

"If Katrinka should need to come over on business," she said, "maybe I could be of some help. I know she doesn't speak French. Besides, I think of her as a friend."

This seemed like a perfectly safe thing to say. Especially since Morgan had already turned down the suggestion once before. Besides, Hetty didn't want him to think she felt threatened. She said, "You'll always be working with her. We can't have business affected just because you get the impression I don't *want* you to."

Morgan said, "It was good of her to call. But about the perfume business—I'd rather take care of it myself. You know why."

"Because she's too . . . pushy?"

Morgan delayed his response, then smiled and made an admission. "And I was trying so hard not to say the word."

They knew Troy was waiting for them in his room, so Hetty and Morgan shortened their conversation and knocked on Sophie's door. Sophie and Stewie followed them without hesitation. When they arrived at Troy's room, the closet door was gaping open, two pairs of shoes were in the middle of the floor, and one bed was rumpled—probably where L. B. had been resting. Troy didn't appear to notice any of this; however, Sophie straightened the room without fanfare and spread the food out on the luggage rack.

"This is real neat!" said Stewie. "Kind of like a picnic. How come we've been eating in the dining room?"

According to Miko, her father was exhausted from chaperoning the two of them around Paris and would remain in his room.

Kenzo wore a black suit and tie for the occasion. He spoke little English, and Miko was busy interpreting, yet she appeared to revel in smoothing over the constant misinterpretations.

Kenzo held up the apple he was eating. "Guudu appuru!" he said cheerfully.

"Mine's good too," said Miko.

When Sophie sliced the gouda cheese in wedges, Kenzo's face lit up with another endorsement. "Guudu gouda cheezu!" he said. "Oishi."

Miko laughed at his joke and explained, "Oishi means delicious."

The time passed pleasantly, then after a while, Kenzo asked, "Tomaado?"

"You want a tomato?" Stewie asked.

Miko explained, "He's wondering about *tomorrow*."

Kenzo was clearly impressed with Miko's interpretive powers. He nodded. "Hai. Tomaado."

Miko said, "Kenzo and I want to go walking tomorrow, but I'm not sure Father will have the energy by then."

Hetty had the distinct feeling she and Morgan would need to play chaperone in Mr. Kawada's place, so before separating, they made the necessary plans.

L. B. appeared ready to rest on one of the beds. As Hetty and Morgan were leaving, Sophie bustled around the room, cleaning up like a contented hostess.

Back in their room, Morgan wasted no time in announcing he had come to a decision. "You're right, Hetty. I was watching Sophie and Miko tonight, and I realized every woman needs to fulfill a meaningful role. I know it's different for each person."

Hetty went to Morgan and tightened her arms around him. She was grateful he understood her needs at last. All the paperwork was ready to send to the registrar of the law school. Soon they would have experiences in common like never before.

He held her away and looked in her eyes. "I love you, Hetty, and I admire your insights."

She thanked him with a kiss. Apparently, he took pleasure in her gratitude, for he prolonged the moment.

"I've just been thinking of myself," he said.

"I'm sure you haven't, Morgan. I do understand your perspective. But it's going to be wonderful. You'll see." Hetty knew this would draw them even closer.

He laughed. "Oh, I wouldn't say that. If it works, it's only because of your unselfishness. It wasn't my idea. After all, it's our honeymoon. Every time my father has mentioned it, I've refused."

"What do you mean about your father?"

"He doesn't see how . . . *assertive* she can be."

"Who . . .?"

"My father. He thinks like you. He says if we don't bring her over here, we'll never know what she's capable of doing." Morgan kissed Hetty's forehead and ran his thumb over the place her hair came to a peak in the middle. "You wanted me to do the right thing, and I love you for it. Now we'll see if Katrinka can really play a meaningful role."

Hetty felt the room spin. *Katrinka* . . . She held tight to Morgan and buried her face in his shoulder. Immobilized by the shock, she clung to him until she could stand on her own.

CHAPTER NINE

Secret Misery

Hetty straightened her spine and walked down the hall to see Miko. Katrinka would be coming to Paris, and Hetty had no one to blame but herself. It was a disastrous misunderstanding between her and Morgan—a disaster with no solution. To keep her misery a secret from Morgan, she would have to avoid speaking of it. Planning the next day's sightseeing activities might be a helpful diversion.

When Miko opened the door, her eyes were shining with excitement. There was so much she wanted to tell Hetty.

"There's protesting in Tokyo," she said. "It's mostly students. The mobs are demonstrating at the U.S. Embassy, and the army's everywhere."

"What's the problem?"

"It's called Anpo. It's like a battle between prewar and postwar Japan. And people don't like Prime Minister Kishi's contempt for democracy."

Hetty failed to see the joy in such dreadful news until Miko explained.

"I had no idea what danger Kenzo went through to meet me!" she said. "His trip to the airport was the most hazardous part. The farmers are furious because the government took their land to build it. He had to dodge mobs and hide around corners to reach the plane. And then the flight took fifty-two hours. Tokyo to Anchorage to Hamburg to Paris."

Miko stopped to take a breath. "He's amazing! When I go there, Kenzo wants to hire a bodyguard to protect me. Don't you think he's handsome? Father's grooming him to take his place in the company . . . says he's an expert on Akoya pearls. To get permission to come, Kenzo had to apply to some travel bureau and prove he was coming on business. That's why he and Father talk about pearls all the time."

Hetty laughed at the energy behind Miko's praise. "I think you like him more than you expected."

Miko blushed. "Well, mostly I've been listening to him talk with Father about the pearl business. But maybe I'll get to know him better tomorrow. I suspect that's my father's plan, and he's just pretending to be tired. Father says Kenzo is from a very traditional family. He's such a gentleman—kind of like the Japanese version of Morgan, don't you think?" Miko's excitement continued to bubble over. "None of my friends have been so formal and reserved. But we'll be living with his mother, and he thinks I'll learn whatever I need to know from her."

"Maybe so," said Hetty, "but I imagine he'll need to learn a lot from you."

Miko appeared more subdued. "Well, I'm not sure it works that way in Japan," she said.

Hetty changed the subject. "Where should we go tomorrow? The Metro could take us almost anywhere. You might be interested in the Notre Dame Cathedral . . . or Monet's home and gardens. The train trip to Giverny would be longer, but Kenzo could enjoy the setting without any translation."

The decision was made—they would set out for Giverny early in the morning.

Hetty was determined to love every moment of every day before Katrinka's arrival.

Dignity

The morning light filtered through the lace curtains. Hetty knew the alarm was due to ring at any moment. Turning over in bed, she whispered in Morgan's ear, "Are you awake?"

"I'll have to check with myself." He smiled and pulled Hetty's arm across his chest. "Something on your mind?"

"Yes, it's about Kenzo. Last night I asked Miko what we should know about him. It sounds like her biggest worry is about her own conduct. She says Japanese girls aren't supposed to laugh aloud or even show their teeth. Anyway, she's nervous about what impression she'll make on him.

"You can't believe all the things she has to keep in mind— like whether she looks symmetrical enough. I guess putting your weight on one leg looks ill-mannered to the Japanese. And she'll need to appear slightly pigeon-toed, because that's considered more feminine. I don't want to appear rude, but I'm not sure I can follow her example."

"Don't worry. He'll understand the cultural differences. All we can do is our best."

Hetty sighed. "I could never be a Japanese wife."

"Is that a promise?" He kissed the palm of her hand.

They dressed in traveling clothes and comfortable walking shoes to meet Miko. When the three of them knocked on Kenzo's door, he bowed and said, "Ohayo!" He soon tried again. This time in his best English. "Guudu moruning." He looked rather dapper in his black suit and tie. But after noticing Morgan's casual shirt and trousers, he said, "Chotto matte, kudasai," and went back in.

"He says he'll be just a minute." Miko whispered, "Do I look all right?"

Hetty assured her she looked especially pretty.

When Kenzo returned with a large briefcase, he was ready to go.

They traveled by Metro to catch the train. At the Saint-Lazare train station, couples all around them were saying their farewells in a most conspicuous manner. Public demonstrations of affection were unheard of in Japan, so Miko knew the sight of people kissing would be offensive to Kenzo. Rather than expose him to anything so awkward, they kept their distance.

Their seats on the train were spacious and comfortable. While Morgan read some information about Giverny, Hetty leaned against the window. After watching the hedgerows whiz by a moment or two, she dozed off with little regard for her symmetry.

Shortly, she heard what sounded like a zipper, but she thought little of it. She was half awake and stirred with the intention of rearranging herself more symmetrically on the seat. As she did so, her eyes opened.

Nothing could have prepared her for the shock of what she saw. Kenzo was standing at his seat undoing his trousers. He had unzipped them, and his belt was off. Balancing artfully, he removed one leg at a time. He seemed to be searching for a coat hook that did not exist. His stocking feet were on a newspaper. Apparently, he had spread it on the floor to keep his clothes clean while he changed.

Miko's face was beet-red, and she kept her hands locked together in her lap. Morgan was gazing intently at something imaginary. The other passengers stared in disbelief.

Hetty could only hope this was not real. With only her peripheral vision, she could tell Kenzo was removing his tie, taking off his cufflinks, and unbuttoning his shirt. Soon he was standing in only his underwear. At the snap of his briefcase, she trained her eyes on the floor, but the spectacle continued to fascinate her.

Soon he was fully dressed in casual shirt and trousers. While the other passengers watched with open mouths, Kenzo carefully folded his suit and packed it in the briefcase. Then after placing it overhead, he returned to his seat.

All with the dignity of a true gentleman.

Ripples

Giverny was more beautiful than Hetty had expected, and the gardens were riotous with color.

Monet's house reminded her of the cottage and its warm, homey feeling. A sudden nostalgia came over her. She could picture each room of their future home—the inviting corner retreats; unexpected stairways and fireplaces; and windows that opened onto small flower patches.

When they stopped at an archway dripping with clematis vines, Morgan asked, "Does this remind you of anything?"

Once again Hetty could envision the cottage and the roses trailing along the white picket fence. They could sit under the trellis and listen to birds calling from the woods.

Hetty longed to start life at home with Morgan.

"But won't the cottage feel too small?" she asked.

"No. All the better to find you."

Monet's dining room was a glorious bright yellow, and the walls were covered with works by famous Japanese artists. Hetty wondered what Kenzo thought of it.

He and Miko talked quietly between themselves, but much of their time was spent in the gift shop. Miko had already explained *omiyage* to Hetty. It was an elaborate custom of gift-giving—almost a way of life. After any trip, it was necessary to return with souvenirs for all friends and family back home in Japan.

On the whole, their return train trip was far less eventful than the earlier one, and the ride was most pleasant. All the souvenir gifts fit tidily under the seats, and Kenzo's briefcase remained closed. Miko sat with her hands centered on her lap, but whenever she smiled, her hand covered her teeth. Kenzo's speech was so animated, and their conversation so lively, that Miko spent a lot of the time hiding behind her hand.

Though it was difficult to express meaningful thoughts, Hetty felt all their conversations conveyed a good-natured friendliness. Exploring each other's languages was delightful in itself, though Hetty doubted she and Morgan would remember any Japanese at all, by morning.

They returned to the hotel before dark and waited for Miko and Kenzo to disappear into their respective rooms.

The minute they were alone, Morgan said, "They'll turn on the city lights soon."

Hetty was eager to watch it happen too, so they decided to follow the street toward the left bank of the river. On their way out, they passed the front desk and discovered a letter addressed to Morgan. He inspected the envelope at length.

"My father has never written to me before."

Hetty could only guess at Morgan's emotions. He appeared to stiffen, and his features took on the stern, chiseled look of Max Morganthal. There was something elegant and majestic about them both. Hetty had grown to love Morgan's parents, and after a long, complicated history between father and son, she dreamed of a reconciliation between them.

Morgan had long hoped for some change, after the years of his parents' disinterest. Above all Hetty knew the desire for his father's approval was based on a genuine respect.

She watched him run his fingers over the envelope, then place it unopened in his pocket. He would read it all in good time.

The bridge seemed like the best place from which to watch the lights. On their way there they strolled past a little antique shop, and a display in the window caught Hetty's eye.

"Morgan, do you like that desk set? The bronze one with the bird on the inkwell? It has a letter holder and a pen tray."

Morgan looked at it for a polite length of time. "It looks nice," he said. "But I think it's for a lady's desk." He turned to walk away.

"I've never seen one like it," she said. "Do you think we could ask about it?"

He was looking ahead toward the bridge and didn't seem to hear.

"I just . . . I just thought it was pretty."

But that was that. Morgan was ready to move on. The letter must be weighing on his mind.

"Do you think they enjoyed the day?" he asked.

What was Morgan talking about? She wanted him to say, *yes, let's get that set for your desk.* But they didn't own a lady's desk, and Hetty knew they never would.

She didn't want to change the subject, but she did, because it seemed selfish to think about a desk set at a time like this.

"I'm not sure," she said. "Miko never looked relaxed. The entire trip seemed like hard work—she had to do so much translating. And being on trial with each other must be a strain."

"Yes," he said. "On the other hand, their parents have probably worked out any important issues ahead of time. There are advantages to such arrangements. Maybe their marriage will be based on wisdom rather than foolish attraction."

What was he saying? Hetty hoped Morgan didn't consider her a mistake. She mustn't analyze his statement. She blinked and watched his fingers run over the letter.

"I hope so," she said. "They do seem compatible."

The lamps on the bridge lit up as they crossed over the river. They stopped to watch the quiet ripples spread spots of light across the water, and Morgan put his arm around her waist.

What effect might the letter have? This one and only letter from his father was sure to cause ripples, and Hetty wanted Morgan to be happy with the contents.

An amorous couple passed them and stopped nearby. Kenzo would have blushed at the sight of them. She and Morgan turned their backs to offer the couple some degree of privacy, whether or not they cared.

Morgan said, "Some people call it the City of Love." He took her hand and looked down at the water.

Hetty respected her husband's public refinement and felt glad for it.

The Letter

They sat on the edge of the bed. Morgan tapped the letter against his knee, as if stalling for the courage to open it. Taking a penknife from his pocket, he slit the envelope carefully and removed it with unsteady hands. The unfolding seemed to take forever.

"What?" he whispered. He read it again. This time, aloud.

> Morgan:
>
> My will and related trust documents previously provided that aspects of your inheritance were conditioned on your marrying Katrinka.
>
> I no longer see a need for those provisions. As of today's date, I have had them deleted from the documents.
>
> It has become obvious to all parties involved that your marriage to Hetty was based on a love of long standing, through numerous tests and challenges.
>
> I was determined to make that fact absolutely clear, as my marriage to your mother suffered because she and others wondered if I chose her for money. For that purpose, I kept the condition in place even as you and Hetty were making plans.
>
> At our invitation, Katrinka will continue to live here in the gatehouse. Your mother and I appreciate your concurrence.
>
> Respectfully,
> Your father, Max

Enclosed are copies of the documents.

"Do you know what this means?"

Hetty put her head on his shoulder. It meant a lot of things. At last Morgan would have an improved relationship with Max. It was of little significance that his letter sounded brusque. They were accustomed to his father's blunt manner.

"This is all your doing, Hetty." Morgan's expression softened with gratitude.

"Not really." She laughed and kissed his cheek.

"Oh yes, it is! Everywhere you go, you make people think better of each other." He danced her around the room. "What is it about you?"

They looked at the letter again and saw things they hadn't noticed the first time.

"The rascal!" Morgan laughed. "He was putting us through a test the whole time."

"It looks that way. Tests and challenges to guarantee you'd be happy."

"I'll go and try calling him. It's afternoon there." He looked over the enclosed documents first, then hurried downstairs.

Twenty minutes later, Morgan returned to the room. His joy was apparent.

"I had a good talk with Dad. Short, but friendly. He's taking Mom to Bermuda and Barbados, among other places. They both send you their best personal regards."

They laughed together at his father's formality.

Suddenly, Hetty had a sinking feeling. The thought of being so rich made her fear unwanted changes in their lifestyle.

"Now that we can afford it," she asked, "will you want a bigger house?"

He hesitated. "Why? Is that what *you* want?"

"I . . . I was just asking."

"This letter won't have to change where we live," he said.

Hetty was relieved to learn the cottage would always be the home of his dreams.

"Something else," he said. "Dad's sending Katrinka here to Paris. But you won't need to deal with her. I'll handle her myself."

Morgan held her tight, then swung her around the room.

Hypocrisy

Katrinka would soon arrive to disrupt their honeymoon, but Hetty and Morgan decided on one final spree before meeting her at the airport.

They attended a matinee performance of *The Misanthrope*. Though neither of them understood enough French to discuss it in any depth, they did know it was about hypocrisy. Morgan was sure his mother would be excited about anything performed at the famous *Comédie Française*.

Morgan's efforts to draw close to his parents pleased Hetty immensely. At first the Morganthals had frightened her, but all that was over now, and she loved them dearly.

She wondered if Max and Mimi had put Katrinka on the plane. Or did the chauffeur take her to the airport? Not only was Katrinka connected with the business, but now she was permanently installed on the Morganthal estate.

To complicate matters, someday soon Morgan would leave for Germany. Hetty had sought every excuse to be close to him. Each moment was a gift magnified by a sweet sadness, and love heightened her awareness of his every virtue.

His sentiments seemed to match hers, so without making any explanation, they rarely spent time in the company of others.

Hetty thought of her grandmother. When she was dying, she made every day count, knowing it could be her last. Hetty sighed, and her mind wandered.

I mustn't dramatize the situation in my head—nobody's dying, for heaven's sake! And I owe it to Katrinka to think the best of her. Any other attitude would be childish. We won't have much to do with each other, anyway. But she doesn't speak any French, so she may need a little help getting around.

She handled the meeting well with Commander Slubbet, but I hope she won't talk about him anymore.

When I last heard, Joseph Ostler was courting Katrinka. What she needs is someone who cares about her, now that she can't run to her father. Or to Morgan.

The plane would be late, and Hetty couldn't help wondering whether Katrinka was somehow responsible. Maybe she was posing for pictures against the plane. It wouldn't be her first time as the center of attention. Perhaps the pilot had let her sit on his lap to play with the little buttons and knobs.

These were unkind thoughts, and Hetty knew better.

They had just passed a little kiosk selling flowers, so she excused herself to go back and buy Katrinka a pink rose. When Morgan expressed appreciation for her thoughtfulness, Hetty knew it was undeserved. Mostly she had done it with the hope of improving her own attitude, but she kept the reason to herself.

I'm living a lie, she thought. *A hypocrite . . . that's what I am.*

Morgan faced her. "Thank you for coming to the airport," he said. "There's something else I need you to do. And I apologize for asking."

"Anything at all," she said. And she meant it.

"It's about Katrinka. Do you think you could watch over her?"

Hetty wondered why his plans had changed. "But I don't know a thing about the French perfume business!" she said.

"You don't have to. I'll be touring the factory with her when I get back. I have to take the overnight train to Germany. My bags are packed."

Hetty blinked. Could this be true?

His explanation was quiet. "Our week together has been perfect. I didn't want to spoil it by telling you."

Hetty saw his sincerity, but what else? Sympathy? She wanted to feel his arms around her, and hoped he felt the same. Something deep inside her was crying out for comfort. But she would not be an object of pity. It was time for her to grow up.

"That was thoughtful," she said, "and it should be fun to have Katrinka here while you're gone. Do you plan to finalize the Ferris wheel contract?"

Before he could answer, Katrinka appeared. There was no mistaking her. In a cloud of perfume, she flounced toward them.

"Morgan, darling! And our sweet Hetty!" She beckoned to a photographer and whispered, "Didn't I tell you?"

"Hetty, do be a dear and hold my little purse."

In the commotion, she threw herself against Morgan, and a camera flashed.

"Oh, dear!" She giggled and moved quickly away. "I didn't mean to trip."

Morgan glared at the cameraman, who disappeared quickly into the crowd.

Maybe Katrinka really did trip.

A crowd gathered to admire the gorgeous couple. Were they movie stars? Judging by the number of suitcases, they must be important. The intrusion of the tall skinny girl was puzzling, but of course, her identity was of no interest.

Katrinka was more beautiful than Hetty remembered. her smooth complexion was radiantly creamy, and her long, lustrous eyelashes fanned the air artfully. For the benefit of all onlookers, she played her dimples. She winked, then blew a kiss to someone in uniform. Was it the captain?

Her lips opened to reveal a row of perfect, pearly white teeth. With the sweetest innocence, she reached toward Morgan to put her arm through his. Instead, Hetty smiled and placed the pink rose in Katrinka's one hand. In the other, she placed the little purse.

Hetty tried to like her.

You're So Lucky

Bottles of lotions, face cream, and makeup remover were lined up in front of the mirror.

"Hetty honey, while Morgan's away I plan to make you look, you know, as pretty as possible. Beauty is a gift you owe your loved ones. That's the motto I live by."

"And even if you're too tall . . . I mean just because you have to look down to see people, you can still hold your chin up. Otherwise, the overhead lights make you look old." She tilted her face heavenward. "See how it gets rid of those unflattering shadows?"

Hetty failed to see what she was talking about, but she nodded and said, "Oh, yes."

The demonstration was quite entertaining. Besides, it seemed like a friendly thing for two girls to do.

Katrinka removed her false eyelashes and placed them in a little pink case labeled *Fanatalash*. "Don't tell anybody," she said with a confidential whisper, "but I don't use our LuvCon lashes. I *tell* people I do, but I'm allergic to the glue."

The process looked frightful to Hetty. "Doesn't it hurt?"

"No, but if it did, it would still be worth it," she said, applying cold cream in upward spirals. "*Never, ever* drag your delicate facial skin down." She made Hetty promise she would never make such a dreadful mistake. With all the cosmetics removed, Hetty thought Katrinka's face was prettier than before. But she doubted her own judgment and simply thanked her for the advice.

Katrinka smiled sweetly. "It's the least I could do! You're such a darling to let me stay with you. I would've been absolutely *miserable* in Uncle Kat's apartment. It's so far from anything fashionable."

Katrinka donned a pink silk cap to protect her curls. "This is my newest product. We must look pretty while we sleep. But I can't teach you everything at once." She smiled indulgently. Hetty blushed to think how primitive her nighttime routine must seem to Katrinka—and maybe to Morgan.

Tilting her head sweetly, Katrinka looked thoughtful for a moment and said, "About what happened at the airport, I hope you'll forgive me. I mean the way I posed with Morgan. Me coming here—you don't know how big it can be for LuvCon! If only we get the right publicity. We've simply *got* to make a splash!"

Katrinka winked at Hetty. "The French love a romance. And what could be more romantic than two gorgeous people in Paris? The public will never know whether we're a couple or not. And knowing Morgan, the only way to pull it off was, you know, to . . . accidentally trip." She laughed sweetly. "Will you forgive me?"

"Yes . . . yes, I understand."

"Then it's our little secret?"

"I don't know . . . I'm not fond of keeping secrets."

"Of course not, honey. It's just that we would *never* want Morgan to think I was being forward! Especially since we're going to be working together so closely."

Katrinka touched a dainty fingertip to her lips. "Someday you'll learn how important *trust* is between a husband and wife. The best way to keep Morgan believing in you is to make sure he doesn't think we tricked him."

The logic behind Katrinka's brand of trust was oddly amusing. And Hetty considered challenging her usage of the word *we* but decided to let it pass.

She tried to trust Katrinka, but with limited success.

A vivid childhood memory came to her. One of her greatest pleasures had been observing birds at the birdfeeder. The black-capped chickadees and nuthatches came throughout the winter. And in the summer, she watched a pair of cardinals take turns feeding their young.

One morning, she was puzzled to see no birds at all. But gradually, within the hour, their numbers increased. When the feeder was once again buzzing with activity, a cat attacked with lightning speed. It came from nowhere, then ran off with the mother cardinal fluttering in its jaws.

For the beautiful cat, it was a just a game of patience and skill, but for the little family of cardinals, it meant life or death.

The memory had stayed with Hetty, and the sadness returned to her now. Was Katrinka waiting and watching for her chance to come in for the kill?

Hetty tried to control her thoughts and was reassured a moment later when Katrinka spoke with gentle concern.

"Hetty dear, please tell me . . . what are your plans now?"

"Well, we have some Japanese friends. They've invited Morgan and me to visit them. It's partly personal but about business too."

"Yes, I know. Pearl powder." She sighed and took Hetty's hand. Her eyes were large and suddenly filled with tears.

"I have some bad news. I didn't want to cause trouble by telling you while Morgan was still here. He would be absolutely *furious* about me telling you. Anyway, I saw something in the newspaper when I was on the plane."

Katrinka brightened as she continued. "The person next to me was smoking a real stinky cigarette, so I went upstairs to the dining room. They were serving prime rib, and this darling man next to me was reading the paper.

"You know me, I give the impression of being bashful, but I *did* have the courage to look over his shoulder. After all, it was our local newspaper. He was having lobster, which looked almost as good as my prime rib. Anyway, he let me tear a piece out of his newspaper. I didn't get the *whole* thing, because on the back there was this article he was saving about us getting another star on the flag. If we've got to add a foreign country, I'm glad it's Hawaii!"

Katrinka's eyes fluttered, and she suddenly covered her face with her hands.

"Oh, Hetty . . . I would do anything to spare you this! You *must* go to Japan with Morgan! Right away, before he finds out."

She fumbled in the pocket of her negligee and pulled out a small, tattered scrap of newspaper.

Hetty held it under the light. Nothing could have prepared her for what she saw.

It read, *The marriage between Morgan Morganthal and Hetty Lawrence is therefore presumed invalid.*

"How could this happen to my dearest friends!" said Katrinka. She uttered little sobs of sympathy.

Hetty thought there must be some mistake. Of course, there had to be a rational explanation. Morgan would straighten it out quickly, upon his return. Meanwhile, she would stay busy, to keep it out of her mind.

Over the next few days, Katrinka did her best to provide distractions. They ate sticky pastries and poked in dress shops together. Hetty wanted Katrinka's opinion of the desk set, so they looked in the window of the antique shop. It was no longer there, and the man inside couldn't remember it.

Perhaps Hetty had wanted it more than she realized. Or maybe it was just the last straw. Whatever the reason, she dissolved in tears on the way home.

I mustn't care about something that can't love me back, she thought. Then she laughed at her own foolishness, but Katrinka didn't laugh at all. Instead, she patted Hetty's arm.

"I know, I know," she whispered, "I feel your pain."

That evening, Hetty suggested having dinner with their other friends, but they were all occupied. Katrinka didn't want to meet them anyway, preferring to spend the evening in lively conversation with Hetty.

"About Commander Slubbet," she said, "I didn't know what he wanted when I first got there. Then I figured it out. He was hoping to find out some dirt about Morgan. But, of course there isn't any, which got him all frustrated.

"He's a married man, but he's no gentleman. Maybe it's my own fault, because when I told him Morgan was a real straight arrow, I guess he thought I was complaining." Katrinka glowered. "That's when it happened. He pulled me toward him and said, 'I bet you didn't always like it that way.' And that made me real mad."

Hetty looked down. "I know it wasn't your fault."

Katrinka continued. "I didn't tell Morgan about that part—it seemed yucky to say such a thing when he admired the commander so much. Besides, I didn't think he'd believe me."

"I'm sure he would have believed you."

But Katrinka shook her head. "Oh, I don't know. It's not like he would have run into anything like that before. And I know you haven't either. You're not the type men act *that way* with, if you know what I mean."

Her expression was suddenly sad and thoughtful. "But wasn't it odd," she said, "when Morgan and I made such a beautiful couple, that he didn't take that into consideration—I mean that he chose you instead. Everybody was shocked."

Katrinka made some unnecessary adjustments to her flawless hairdo with her long pink fingernails and tossed her head as if to show she had recovered her pride.

"People assume beautiful women *like* being attractive to men. It's really just a burden. You're so lucky to be . . . well, not burdened in that way."

Hetty tried to feel lucky, but found it challenging, under the circumstances.

CHAPTER TEN

Ball and Chain

If anyone felt lucky, it was Morgan Morganthal. He would soon see Hetty—and as if that wasn't enough to make him smile, the Ferris wheel negotiations had been successful. The details would have to be put in writing later, but they had agreed to all the terms with a handshake.

The entire legal battle would interest Hetty, and he couldn't wait to tell her about it. At the train station, he called her to say he would be there as soon as possible. But first, Katrinka was waiting for him at the perfume factory. He had to go straight there and tour it with her.

Morgan felt even better after washing his face in the men's room. With a glance in the mirror, he thought, *Now there's a happy man!*

The weather was perfect, and the taxi driver's mood seemed to match his own. Though Morgan couldn't make sense of the man's jokes, laughing together was the whole fun of it. They arrived at their destination cheerfully and on time.

Morgan was greeted at the door by the president of the company and the factory supervisor. Katrinka's advance preparations were so impressive that Morgan considered her with a new respect and admiration.

Why should I be surprised at how cordial and professional she is? Katrinka's a smooth operator in every way.

Both of their hosts spoke understandable English, but the translator was helpful anyway. At the end of two informative hours, he left Morgan and Katrinka on a bridge overlooking the laboratory. Morgan was uncomfortable being alone with Katrinka and hoped the translator would soon rejoin them.

Their conversation began with Katrinka showing a genuine interest in his work. "If Daddy was still alive, he would have loved traveling with you."

"I miss your father," said Morgan. "I always valued his advice. In Czechoslovakia, the Kludskys knew about his death. They see it as a tremendous loss to the circus world."

"I know," she sighed. "I'll always be grateful you took care of his funeral. I couldn't have managed it alone. And it must've cost Max a fortune!"

Morgan did have something to discuss with Katrinka. Maybe this would be a reasonable time.

"Katrinka, about our financial arrangement—the one we had before . . ."

"You mean the one where we would have both been rich if you'd married me?"

He flushed. "Yes, of course it has to be different now, but we all want you to be happy in the gatehouse."

The silence that followed was not typical of the Katrinka he knew, and Morgan felt it was not going well. He tried not to gasp for air, for fear of revealing his guilty feelings. A sense of responsibility, however undefinable, would always be there.

"And if anything develops between you and Joseph," he said, "it goes without saying, we would want him to feel just as welcome."

Again, she seemed to hide behind a professional mask. Morgan would do the same, if that's what she wanted. "Your understanding of the business is impressive," he said. "I'd like to see the publicity proposal you mentioned, but I'm confident you can manage the next few days on your own. I need to get back to Hetty."

Katrinka gave him a puzzled look. "Are you saying she's like a ball and chain? I *hope* you don't feel that way! I realize she's pitifully dependent—and she's always getting lost. But in spite of all her faults, I've come to love her like a sister. Besides, when she acts helpless, it's only so you'll think she's kind of cute. It's bound to take time with such an immature girl, but I know you can adjust to this marriage. I'll do anything I can to help."

Katrinka raised her chin with a sudden show of detachment. "Just for the sake of discussion," she asked, "if you were single, do you suppose you would take an interest in me?"

Morgan laughed and said, "Who wouldn't?"

Under the circumstances, such a response seemed almost necessary. Maybe Katrinka's question was a result of some lingering insecurity he had caused.

Besides, he was *not* single and never would be.

Katrinka's eyes shone with compassion, as she volunteered another helpful thought.

"Hetty may not need you as much as you think, bless her heart." She licked her lips. "Otherwise, why would she consider traveling to Tokyo without you?"

That's Insane!

Morgan had to know what was going on. Why wouldn't Hetty want to travel with him? What kind of honeymoon was that?

As he entered their hotel room, she was on the other side of the door ready to go out. His arrival seemed to startle her. Something in her demeanor was unfamiliar. She seemed strangely sad and distant, as if unwilling to see him.

"What is it, Hetty?"

"I was . . . I was just going to meet Miko. Kenzo brought her a beautiful gift from Japan. I haven't seen it yet."

"What's the matter? Katrinka said something about your going to Japan."

He didn't mean to grip her arms so tightly. "Would you really go without me?"

She avoided his eyes by looking at his tie.

Hetty returned to her previous topic. "Miko's afraid he'll want her to wear a kimono all the time. He gave her a pin for where the cord ties over the sash."

Morgan saw her sadness and loosened his grip. "Hetty . . ."

Her eyes filled with tears. But she kept talking, as if hoping he didn't notice.

"And then," she said, "he gave Mr. Kawada a *netsuke*. It's made of whale's tooth."

Hetty's sadness and Kenzo's gifts were unrelated issues, Morgan was sure of it. As he watched her lips form words, he wanted to kiss them and tell her everything would be all right.

"Whale's tooth, you say?"

"I think . . . whale's tooth," she whispered.

Her eyes were soft and confused, and he felt himself melting toward her. Whatever else was wrong, his kiss was gladly received. They were meant to be together. Morgan expected her to say more. He swayed with her, waiting to hear what it was.

Soon she asked a timid question. "Do you think I should try to . . . to make myself look pretty?"

Morgan scowled. Where did Hetty get such a strange idea? The idea of her changing was so upsetting to him that he almost betrayed his annoyance. Beauty, beauty, beauty! He was sick and tired of it. He wanted her to stay exactly as she was. He wondered if Katrinka had anything to do with it.

Hetty's quizzical expression required an answer.

Morgan felt an overpowering appreciation for all she meant to him—for the beauty of her unquestioning love and trust. He realized none of that could be put into mere words.

Overwhelmed with gratitude, he kissed her again. Love was the answer, and the power of it made his heart swell. Love and light were all around them and seemed to lift them together.

Maybe his instincts were correct, because Hetty seemed to have a renewed confidence. Taking his hand, she guided him to sit with her at the side of the bed. Looking directly into his eyes, she said, "You know how much I care, don't you? And you know no matter how much I love you, I couldn't enjoy our . . . our intimacy if we weren't married."

"Of course not."

"So, I need to tell you something . . . something I wish I didn't know. It's possible we're not legally married."

"What do you mean?"

"Katrinka saw it in the newspapers."

"What? That's insane! She must be wrong. She has no right to say something like that!"

"But she does if it's true."

Hetty showed him the clipping and continued. "I guess it's not uncommon. When a minister is less experienced, it can happen. The ceremony, the marriage license, and the minister's permit all have to be issued in the same state, or some such thing. I don't understand how it works. It was different when we didn't know. Now I've told you, and we can't either of us claim ignorance. When we pledged our whole selves to each other, didn't we mean our whole *best* selves?"

"Yes, our integrity . . ."

"And to uphold the law."

Down at the front desk Morgan tried to phone anyone who had been involved with their wedding, but after a string of bad connections, he had no success. Either he reached people unable to help him, called the wrong numbers, or got disconnected. Hetty's father, the one most able to solve it, could not be located. Further attempts turned up no encouraging news whatsoever.

Even though Morgan hesitated to ask his father for help, he felt driven by desperation.

Sadly, according to Swenson the butler, his parents were already somewhere in the Caribbean and left no instructions on how they could be reached. Finding a few phone numbers from the Morganthals' Rolodex, Swenson offered to make some calls himself. One of the people for whom Morgan left messages might respond, if they were lucky.

He dreaded telling Hetty such discouraging news, but she was waiting for the results with an optimistic smile. He felt like a heel.

The details he explained were meant to show he had been thorough, but it had the effect of convincing them both there was little hope.

"That's not the half of it," he said. "I talked to the American Consulate. To get married in France, we'd need to provide proof of residency—for thirty days."

Morgan was downhearted and knew he couldn't hide it. He had made a complete mess of their honeymoon.

Hetty smiled. "Is there *anyone* you haven't called?"

"Yes, the dogcatcher."

The Chaperone

Hetty and Morgan knew they would need separate rooms now, but the hotel had no vacancies. There was an extra bed in Katrinka's room, but that was the one solution Hetty hoped to avoid. Instead, she approached Sophie, hoping it might be all right to move in with her for a short time.

Sophie was tactful enough not to ask why. She said, "I'm so sorry—especially after you were so kind to let me stay with you. Stewie would love to move out and room with Troy again, but I'm afraid it wouldn't work."

Hetty remembered why and finished Sophie's thought. "L. B. has to stay with Troy sometimes, doesn't he?"

"Yes, and I can see he needs him right now. I wonder if he always will. I see Troy in a whole new light when he's with his brother."

Judging from Sophie's expression, the light in which she saw Troy must have shown him to great advantage. Sophie continued. "Stewie wants to discuss his birthday plans with Morgan. He has a strange idea how to celebrate, but he thinks the men will go along with it. Troy's too involved with L. B. right now. Stewie has become attached to him, and he'll be terribly disappointed if Troy's too busy to be involved."

Sophie's next comment came as a surprise. "I think you see right through me, don't you, Hetty?" She didn't seem to expect an answer. "I feel guilty about . . . well, I never should have married Ben. Everyone knows it was for convenience. Do you think Troy could ever be interested in someone with such low standards?"

"It wasn't entirely for convenience. You had a mutual agreement. You cared for Ben, and it made him happy."

Sophie shook her head. "I shouldn't have concealed it."

"But you had no choice. It was Ben's idea. Why not discuss it with Troy?"

Hetty was revisiting the front desk about getting a room when she heard a sweet, musical voice behind her. It was Katrinka.

"You need a chaperone, don't you, honey? Why don't you stay with me?"

The cat had come to pounce.

Approval

Hetty and Morgan were about to leave for the Louvre. They had already been there twice and planned on going back as often as possible. However, at the last minute, Morgan decided to stay behind at the hotel, where he could be reached by phone.

Katrinka wondered why *anyone* would want to see such a place. It was nothing but a huge, famous museum with all kinds of artwork. But Hetty was pleased that Miko wanted to join her. In the Metro station on the way there, they saw a group of street musicians with an excellent violinist. When they stopped to listen, it was clear Miko had come primarily to talk. Their conversation took the very direction Hetty had been expecting.

"When I had to break up with John, I thought I'd never recover. It seemed so unfair for Father to disapprove without meeting him. I really like Kenzo, but I would probably like him better if I'd met him on my own. Why should it matter if I follow my father's wishes?"

Hetty had a ready response. "I've always admired the respect Japanese children show for their parents."

Miko's surprise was evident. "I thought you were a more independent woman."

Hetty laughed. "I don't think respect and independence are mutually exclusive."

She thought about her violin. Though her father wished her to play duets with him, it was just as much her desire. She said, "Of course, it would be better if your wishes and his are the same."

"Is that what it boils down to?"

Hetty sighed. "I don't really think so. It seems like there's a lot more to it than that."

"What do you mean?"

Hetty was reluctant to influence Miko, but she stated her opinion. "Don't you think it helps to have the same goals? And I wonder if a parent can see us more objectively than we see ourselves. But even if you came from the same background, everyone has to adjust." Hetty hoped her ideas sounded balanced enough.

Miko nodded. "Well, I could adjust to the Japanese customs—things like the complicated gift-giving rituals or wearing a kimono. Even people undressing in the train." She laughed.

Hetty thought it more respectful to Kenzo not to react. "But you see other problems?"

"Yes." Miko took a deep breath. "The biggest one is probably corporate life in Japan. I found out my father advanced Kenzo the money to come here. Nobody can bring more than five hundred dollars out of Japan, and it has to be in travelers' checks. The travel bureau only allows people to leave once a year, and it has to be for business. Father paid for Kenzo's plane ticket, and he's promised him a job for life. There are serious obligations between employers and employees."

Hetty had hoped she could remain neutral, but how could she stand by and watch? She thought of how Max Morganthal had tried inducing Morgan to marry Katrinka. Maybe Miko was considered nothing more than a business deal, to the men.

"I can see it's complicated," she said. "I think such an adjustment requires a lot of love. It has to feel worth it, and you're the only one who can decide on that."

"I'm scared," said Miko. "It's a wonder anyone marries."

A problem suddenly occurred to Hetty. Could Katrinka have stayed behind at the hotel deliberately to make trouble? Was she still hoping the company would send her to Japan? If so, she might try to cozy up to Mr. Kawada or Kenzo. There could be other things. Hetty wanted to trust her but wondered if she could.

As soon as they entered the hotel, Hetty could smell a cloud of Katrinka's perfume. Morgan stood frowning at a glossy photograph, which he handed to Hetty.

The picture made her gasp. Katrinka was the central figure and looked radiantly beautiful. She was pressed against a striking gentleman who appeared to focus on the luggage. Anyone could see it was Morgan.

Superimposed on the right foreground was an enlarged bottle of perfume. *Katrinka* by LuvCon.

"She's already sent it out," he said. "She tells me you approved."

The Portfolio Secret

Hetty was not expecting the photograph of Morgan and Katrinka to be so dramatic. There was no hiding her shock, but she thought it best not to make waves. She said only, "I agreed with Katrinka that it should be good publicity, and I did understand the reason for it."

Morgan said, "It's bad timing. I don't want it feeding rumors about our marriage."

Hetty felt the same but said only, "What's done is done." She would try to move on like Morgan always did.

Just then Troy and Sophie approached. They had arranged to meet for dessert, so the four of them sat at a small corner table where they could talk. Morgan spoke before the waiter handed them the menus. "Sophie," he said, "while Hetty was gone I heard back from Jack Anderson. Whatever his sources, we can trust his information. You should be safe.

"Jack learned Ben was no saint, until he met a woman who changed his life—his housekeeper. He says she has a twelve-year-old son." Morgan nodded at Sophie. "And that for her sake, he paid off his debts to . . . let's just call it the underworld. Ben had always gotten around the law, and he kept looking for schemes to make his housekeeper rich. Toward the end, he retained an excellent lawyer who fought to keep him out of trouble—made him do everything legally.

"This attorney was fond of Ben. He called him a rough man with a big heart." Sophie's eyes were wide with surprise.

Troy nodded. "This means you can come and go. And you won't need me to watch over you anymore."

Sophie said, "But I . . . we've really liked it." She averted her eyes.

Hetty could tell Troy liked Sophie's answer. He watched her until she spoke again.

"I'll have to tell Stewie about Ben."

Troy was still watching her, as if mustering the courage to say more. After the crème brûlée and chocolate soufflé had disappeared, he reached behind the seat for his portfolio. He seemed so hesitant to open it that Hetty wondered why he had brought it along.

"Maybe I should . . . I should start by showing you this." he said. "I need to get something off my chest. I only hope you'll forgive me." Troy opened his portfolio. Pointing out a photograph, he said, "This is one of my earliest paintings."

When he passed it to Morgan, Hetty leaned in close to get a better look. It provided an excuse for putting her arm through his. So great was her pleasure in touching him that she failed to notice the significance of the photograph at first.

But soon she said, "So *you're* the artist!" She looked to Troy for some explanation. "Morgan, it's the wonderful, life-size portrait of your mother. Troy's the one who painted it."

Troy said, "Yes, it's Mimi Morganthal. I remember the whole experience. She was already married, but her parents bought that dress and forced her to pose in it."

"Yes," Morgan explained. "My grandparents were socially prominent, and they despised my father for being a clown. So my parents eloped. They told her she wasn't worthy to wear a white dress, then made her do it anyway."

Hetty had long admired the portrait. "The way you painted her face—her features are flawless," she said. "Mimi's still very regal. You captured that perfectly. Even the way she used to look sort of detached."

"Yes. She was crying so much it was hard to paint her face."

Troy shifted awkwardly in his seat and began again. "In my profession, to get commissions we have to connect with people who have the money to pay for them. I knew about your family and who you were. I didn't dare say so. And I knew who Katrinka Wallace was." He faced Sophie. "I was afraid if you knew I was following the Morganthals, you'd think I was after Ben's money too."

Sophie shook her head. "No, I never would."

He watched her still. "I feel better telling you, but I hope no one's offended. I didn't expect Hetty and Morgan to become my good friends. And I didn't know you and Stewie would be important to me the way you are."

His face became quite red, as he spoke softly to Sophie. "You and Stewie make me feel very rich. Because . . . like Hetty says, the more people she loves, the richer she feels."

Not Too Wrinkly

Sophie excused herself to tell Stewie about Ben.

Even if it was time to go, Hetty didn't want to. Morgan had just found her hand under the table. Their decision to have a chaperone always present was a constant misery at best.

Stewie arrived, and Troy said, "You just missed your mom."

"That's okay. I was looking for you. Me and you gotta have a man-to-man talk." He glanced at the Morgathals. "You guys too. You know, like a committee meeting, only important."

He drew himself up like the chairman of the board. "I'm twelve, but that's not as grownup as it sounds. Lots of guys at school got dads. But they aren't, you know, real good at it, I don't guess." He looked directly at Troy and said, "I think you'd be scads better at it than them. I don't have a dad, but like Hetty says, when I think up good ideas, being man of the house, I should say them out loud. So, here's what I think: me and you could both take care of my mom better than if it was just myself." He took a big breath.

"A real nice lady like my mom—I mean she's not too wrinkly or anything—I told her she should get married. Ben says nobody would want her except him—just 'cause she never got married before. Anyway, so why don't *you* marry us?"

Hetty smiled at Stewie—in part because Morgan's ankle was rubbing against hers.

Both amusement and happiness showed in Troy's face. He put his hand on Stewie's shoulder and said, "Maybe your mother should be involved in this decision."

Stewie appeared impressed with Troy's idea. "Yeah, I'll go get her!"

He almost tipped over his chair in his enthusiastic departure.

Troy laughed. "Was it something I said?" His expression became more thoughtful, and he excused himself to wait for Sophie at the entrance of the dining room. She soon arrived without Stewie. Troy took her by the hand to a quiet corner of the lobby.

Hetty stated the obvious and whispered, "It's no typical marriage proposal."

Morgan glanced at her as if remembering their own unusual circumstances. When it happened for them, she had been high in a tree, sobbing in misery about his impending marriage to Katrinka. He climbed to give Hetty her first kiss and accept her startling proposal.

While telling Morgan about her visit to the Louvre, Hetty watched the serious blue of his eyes and waited for the corners of his mouth to turn up in a smile. Sitting with him was so pleasant that she hoped he would never ask for the bill.

Hetty was so deep in the thrall of her husband that she hardly noticed Troy's return.

Troy looked thoroughly defeated, and his explanation was slow and halting. But he seemed in need of listening ears. "I should have known," he said. "It was too good to be true. I was wrong to think it was Sophie's idea. I was hoping she put Stewie up to it."

Hetty could tell he had been humiliated. After a while, he shook his head and said, "It was all Stewie's idea." He turned red with embarrassment as he spoke of it. "I told Sophie that Stewie had a plan, and I wondered how *she* felt about it. That's all I had to say. She knew what I was talking about." Troy stared out the window as if it was awkward to face them.

He sighed and continued. "Sophie doesn't know where Stewie gets such ideas. She'd like to humor him, but the whole thing makes her ill. She thinks he just wants to impress his friends at school. Sophie suggested we could take pictures for show and tell and that would be enough. I couldn't believe it."

Troy made a fist. "I had no idea I made her sick. But I'll tell you what disappointed me most: she says it would be too much trouble for something so trivial. *Trivial,* she called it."

Hetty said, "There must be some misunderstanding."

No words of consolation formed in her mind. The three of them sat brooding over Troy's defeat for a few minutes.

Then Hetty saw a figure out of the corner of her eye. It was Sophie, and she looked quite cheerful—as if nothing had happened.

She came straight to the table. "Troy," she said, "Stewie was sure you'd go along with it. I'll be cringing the whole time, but for his sake I've reconsidered. I'll try to be a good sport and see it from a man's point of view. Really though, would *any* woman like an octopus?"

When she left, Troy looked stunned at her lack of sensitivity.

CHAPTER ELEVEN

Help Arrives

Morgan Morganthal was a man of steady disposition whose moods were normally unaffected by circumstances. However, at this time, he hurt all over with an ill-defined sadness. When going alone to his room for the night, he wanted to avoid seeing anyone on the elevator, so he went by way of the stairs.

Among the many things disturbing him, Morgan kept thinking of what Sophie had said. *How could she talk that way? Troy has always conducted himself as a gentleman. That was an insulting comparison. Hetty would never say anything so unkind.*

In his room, he dragged himself to the bathroom and splashed his face with cold water. He felt no better. His beard was growing in, but he had no one for whom to shave. The mirror reflected the misery he felt.

Hetty had left a blouse in the closet. He held it to his face, drawing comfort from the scent of her.

The city lights were jarring. Their brightness battered his defenses, so he closed the shades. His thoughts became darker.

Lying on the bed, Morgan hoped for a merciful sleep to overtake him. He tried to find answers to his complaints, but instead, they loomed even larger.

I'm afraid if Hetty becomes an attorney, she won't think she needs me anymore, Still, I shouldn't take selfish control. I know better. It's no way to build her confidence.

Most of all, the inheritance feels like a curse. The Morganthal money means I won't be her provider anymore. She must feel she doesn't need me anyway, or she wouldn't be willing to travel alone.

I'm acting like a victim—or a problem in search of a solution. I mustn't think that way.

I couldn't think straight when I was sitting next to her. And I've ruined our honeymoon.

Why hasn't even the county clerk called me back?

And now with Katrinka's publicity stunt, Slubbet will have the ammunition he wants—a scandal about me.

Morgan's misery was getting him nowhere. He gripped the blouse and thought of Hetty. She thought love was the answer to everything. How was she dealing with their situation?

Was that a knock at the door? It couldn't be the housekeeper. She had already changed the towels. He stood and walked slowly to answer it.

It was Hetty, with her cheeks glowing and her pink lips parted in a shy apology. "I'm sorry if you were resting. I just came by to give you my key."

She reached into her pocket. He had to think fast so she wouldn't leave.

"Your key?" He spoke across the doorjamb. "Why's that?"

"I don't want to have it." She dipped her head the way she always did when she was embarrassed. "I mean I *shouldn't* have it."

"That's true," he said. He wanted to tell her he loved her.

He said, "We'll figure this out soon, then you can move back in. So, keep the key."

"It wouldn't be a good idea."

"Why? You don't have to use it."

"Well . . . I might forget and come in here."

"How would that happen?" he asked.

"Maybe, oh . . . for example, if I'm sleepwalking."

"You don't walk in your sleep."

"There's always a first time."

"Why would you?" he asked.

"To come see you. And we can't have people thinking I would."

Morgan agreed, though he was quite excited at the possibility. "But you said you might."

"Might what?" she asked.

"Come see me in the middle of the night," he said. "Why would you?"

"Maybe if I need you to kiss me goodnight?"

"And would I?" he asked.

"Oh, no . . . it could give people the wrong idea."

"What idea do you think people have?" he asked.

"People probably think I'm desperate to be touching you every minute."

"And would they be right?" he asked.

"I won't say." Her eyes said *yes*.

Morgan knew he mustn't keep her any longer; it would only make things harder.

Even though she stepped backward into the hall, her lingering look indicated a reluctance to leave.

"I see you have my blouse," she said.

"Yes, and you left a few things in the bathroom drawer."

"But I haven't missed anything."

"You could check," he said.

Morgan knew he shouldn't have suggested it but was glad he did. Following her into the bathroom, he watched her in the mirror. Her hair floated around her face like milkweed, and he wanted to glory in its softness . . . to feel it swirling all around him.

The drawer was stuck, and she couldn't figure out why. Morgan's hand was too large to reach inside and unstick it. But there must be a way.

While he struggled with it, she stood behind him and encircled his chest with her arms. "Is this helping?" she asked.

He laughed. In order to make the process last longer, he labored only half-heartedly. All the while, he felt his gloom lifting.

They sat on the edge of the bed and wondered if the next people to inhabit the room would like whatever treasures she abandoned.

"Ah, oui," said Morgan. "Mademoiselle Fifi La Lune, she'll be très enchantée."

Hetty's sunburn was still peeling, and Morgan found it quite charming. To get a closer look, he took her face between his hands and shared her sweet breath. Her eyes closed, and he knew everything about her was ready to yield.

Instinct and Remorse

Hetty put her head on Morgan's shoulder. "I should go," she said.

His lips brushed her forehead, her eyelids, her chin.

"Definitely," he said. But they stayed as they were.

As a gift of sweet comfort, she touched his face, and her trembling fingers lingered on the roughness of his cheeks.

It might have been the tiny flecks of gold in his serious blue eyes, the thatch of dark hair falling over his forehead, or the touch of his hand. Whatever it was, she yearned for more, and Morgan was ready to oblige. The power of his warmth and goodness engulfed her.

At dawn, the sun awakened Hetty. Her lip trembled. What had happened could not be undone.

She put her hand in Morgan's. "I know love doesn't make it right. If it did, what were we saving ourselves for, over the years?"

What could he say?

His thumb wiped a tear from her cheek. "You have a kind heart, Hetty. I love you for your instinct . . . for your concern. Please don't feel guilty. It's my fault."

"No, Morgan." A tear ran down her cheek and wet the pillow. "Mostly I feel ashamed about not feeling guilty. Please forgive me. I was pretending to be your wife. I just wanted it to be true," she whispered. "But I'm not sorry I love you."

Morgan kissed her fingers. "I'm acquainted with self-control. I should have used it. This was deliberate on my part."

Hetty was quiet for a time, then said, "Just because it didn't *feel* wrong doesn't mean it wasn't."

He nodded. "That's true. And to claim we couldn't help it . . . that would be like denying the blame."

He rotated her wedding band and kissed her cheek.

"We can do better."

He rose to open the shades. A soft light filtered through the lace curtains, bathing the room in a warm glow.

Hetty knew no sorrow was adequate to excuse their transgression. Only the promise of forgiveness could overcome its darkness. She stood by Morgan, facing the light.

"Let's go home," he said. "There's a way to fix this."

He was right. She put the key in his hand.

It's All Settled

Sophie felt safe leaving the hotel now, so Morgan made reservations for nine at a restaurant down the street. It would be a reunion of sorts. Hetty dressed for dinner in the room she shared with Katrinka, and the two of them walked together to the restaurant.

Hetty and Morgan wanted to fill the remaining days in Paris with the best possible experiences. However, they were going home, and Hetty's thoughts were increasingly on the future. This change also meant their Tokyo plans must be postponed, but they hoped to go in the near future. The Kawadas had graciously renewed their invitation.

Morgan was waiting outside, and Hetty saw him as if with new eyes. Respect and admiration had always been there, but now there was something more profound. A part of her still saw him with the awe and wonder of her earlier years, but now Hetty was a partner in the inner workings of his mind, and she felt honored to be trusted there. Together, they had stumbled through darkness and light to a place of pure love and humility.

Hetty saw Troy and Stewie had already arrived, and both of them looked miserable. Right away she could tell Stewie was hearing the bad news.

Troy said, "So, that's the end of that. I just don't suit your mother's taste."

Sophie arrived next and did the unexpected. Walking straight to Troy, she put her arm through his. To Stewie, she said, "It's all settled. But we might need Mr. Kawada to take us to the fish market. He'll know how much an octopus should cost. The more I thought about it, I want pictures to show *my* friends, too."

For a brief moment, Troy looked from Sophie to Stewie. His eyes were wide with surprise and confusion. "Do I understand what's going on here?"

The three of them spoke together with animation, interrupted with intermittent laughter. When they had cleared up their misunderstanding, they took Morgan and Hetty aside to tell and retell them the story.

Stewie was delighted that his mother had approved of having an octopus at his birthday party. But that was nothing compared to the best news of all.

"Guess what! We're marrying Troy," he announced, "and I arranged it myself."

No one could disagree.

Forthright

Hetty was glad no one seemed to know about their marital status. She gave Katrinka credit for saying nothing about it. Rooming with her was working out just fine, and they got along quite pleasantly. In fact, when Katrinka learned her perfume gave Hetty hay fever, she put it away.

Hetty was thinking of this with gratitude, as Katrinka applied her nighttime creams and ointments. While awaiting her turn at the wash basin, Hetty looked through a recent issue of *Paris Match* magazine. She stopped frequently to check her *Petit Larousse* dictionary, but when she heard a scuffling sound, she put it down. A folded note had come under the door. It was from Morgan, and it read,

> *Heard from Jack Anderson—Slubbet resigning from Ethics Committee! To "spend more time with his wife and family."*
> *Je t'aime big time.*
> *Your M.*

Hetty wondered what might be behind the story. Would they ever learn the answer?

Suddenly it occurred to her that Katrinka might know more. She had a friendship of sorts with Tilly Teller, the gossip columnist. Why not ask her directly?

Hetty sat on the edge of the tub. "About our marriage being illegal—you didn't give that idea to the commander, did you?"

Katrinka looked startled. "How could you think such a thing!" She stared at Hetty's reflection. "To tell the truth, I don't remember *what* I said when I first got there . . . but couldn't he have seen it by then anyway?" She blinked rapidly.

"I mean . . . I bet he already knew. That's it. And I bet he's the one who found out and told the newspapers. I mean, however he found out. And . . . and one thing's for sure—I could *not* tell the commander you *are* married. Because it might not really be true! I mean nobody can swear to *anything* one hundred percent! And you know I wouldn't be able to *live* with myself if I made up something like that."

Katrinka put something on her eyes. Wet cotton balls? Whatever they were, Hetty suspected she did it to avoid making eye contact.

"Yes," said Hetty, "and your father was that way too. Honest in all his dealings. Morgan says he could always count on Phil to be completely forthright."

Katrinka seemed distressed with the discussion of honesty, but no other subject seemed to occur to her at first. After fumbling with the cotton balls, she removed them from her eyes. "Did it ever occur to you maybe it was *meant* to happen this way? It could be a *good* thing. Maybe this little legal mix-up gives us all time to think."

Hetty said, "I don't need time to think."

"Of course. I know how you feel, honey." Her sweet smile hinted at sincerity. "But we need to consider Morgan's feelings too." She tilted her head with sympathy. "I hesitate to tell you this, but to be entirely forthright—like my father—Morgan says if he was single he'd be interested in me again."

Hetty's gaze was steady. "Morgan won't need time to think either. He wants us to be together as much as I do."

"Hetty dear, you're so naïve! If he really wanted to be with you, he would."

A blush crept across Hetty's face. She was glad Katrinka didn't know she had been with Morgan. "Well, I'm . . . I'm just saying he's not available."

Katrinka laughed, "He is if he's not married."

Could Katrinka have started the rumor? Even if she had, what good could come of telling Morgan? Hetty would keep her suspicions to herself. They would be home soon and able to find the truth.

Hetty changed the subject. "How is Joseph?"

Katrinka wiped her face with a little square of pink flannel and said, "Daddy liked Joseph a lot. I've been considering whether to accept his proposal, but he says he'll only marry me if I work my way to Australia by tramp steamer."

Katrinka laughed as if the idea was totally preposterous. Hetty saw her point. How could she maintain her demanding beauty regimen while swabbing the decks and peeling potatoes?

Katrinka continued. "I figure if LuvCon flies me to Japan, then I can go by tramp steamer from there to Australia. As long as I do it for the *final* leg of the trip, he'll never know!"

She winked as if to make Hetty a co-conspirator in her clever plot.

"Would you really do that?" Hetty asked. Hetty and Morgan both considered Joseph a good friend.

The fact that Joseph once courted Hetty was a constant irritant to Katrinka. She frowned and said, "You're not the big expert on Joseph, honey. You just want me to *think* you are. I bet you're trying to point out I'm getting one of your leftovers. We shouldn't even be *having* this conversation! It doesn't make sense for me to be the one ending up alone. Let's be honest—I'm prettier than you.

"And I take real good care of myself. I exfoliate my skin every night and push back my cuticles. And look at *you*. Before long, there won't be anything left of your face, it's peeling so much. Besides, Morgan has no business looking so great, then wasting it all. You make him look short." The tears gathered, but she blinked them away. "We used to look real spectacular together. If you can't see it, you're completely out of touch with reality."

When Katrinka had finished her tirade, she looked dejected.

Hetty said, "You're right about so many things. But you're more than just a pretty face, Katrinka. You're fearless and determined, with a creative mind for business."

"Do you really think so?" Katrinka lifted her chin, and there was a new gleam in her eye.

"Yes, Morgan sees it too. But about the pearl business . . . we're not going to Japan. It's time for us to go home. I know you would like to go without us, but Japan may not be ready for a woman executive."

"Well then, that's exactly why I should go!"

Hetty smiled. "You see? That's what I mean about you."

Before brushing her teeth, Hetty wrote a note to Morgan and slipped it under his door.

> *I love you too,*
> *H.*

Bombs Away!

Morgan arranged for everyone to meet in the hotel dining room. It would be one of the last evenings for them to be together. To Hetty, it meant being with Morgan.

Mr. Kawada was sitting by Hetty. When the others were occupied, he whispered, "My Miko like very much Kenzo. You think is good?"

"He seems like a fine man. But there are lots of cultural differences."

"You think? What differences?"

"Well, like so many American girls, she might expect to be an equal partner with her husband."

"Equal? Like same-same?" He squinted and drew air through his teeth. "Is not possible."

"Let's be honest — I'm prettier than you."

"Oh, not *really* same-same." Hetty smiled. "Different-different, but like partners. American girls like to walk *with* their husbands, not follow behind them."

He turned to Morgan. "You hear what Hetty say? Not behind? I think is hard."

Morgan nodded. "Yes," he said, "but she's right."

Hetty sensed she had surprised Mr. Kawada. Deep in thought, he was watching Miko and Kenzo with curiosity. The two of them were clearly in their own little world and spoke only Japanese. Mr. Kawada looked thoughtful.

After a while, he leaned toward Hetty and whispered, "Why Miko can't decide?"

She had no answer.

After a while, Mr. Kawada grinned and looked around the table as if ready to enact a plan. When all eyes sensed something important would soon happen, he stood and bowed.

"I have big, big announcement!" he said, "and now is time to tell. I think is good Japanese tradition. And very nice surprise for my unworthy daughter. I now present heir to company leadership."

He directed attention to Kenzo, who stood and bowed.

"Kenzo now my adopted son!" He clapped his hands and looked around the table as a signal for the others to applaud as well. His new son and heir continued to bow in gratitude to Mr. Kawada, as the others clapped. The only one not applauding was Miko.

"Bonzai!" said Mr. Kawada, lifting his glass.

Hetty wondered what he meant by that. Was it a way of saying *hooray* or *congratulations?* To her it sounded like *look out, the bombs are falling!* The others appeared to be of the same opinion, but one by one they lifted their glasses.

Mr. Kawada appeared more than satisfied. His conversation continued to sound happy, though it was in Japanese.

He leaned toward Hetty. "Now Miko find more easy to decide, I think. Good future. Prosperous."

Miko stared straight ahead as if stunned. Hetty could only hope she knew her father's idea was not hers or Morgan's.

Apparently, Stewie was not ready to let the excitement end. He was the next one to stand and get everyone's attention. "*I've* got a big announcement, everybody. After this, you all gotta come to *our* party!"

Sophie fidgeted and whispered, "What . . . are you sure?"

Troy looked just as puzzled. But he put his hand on hers, and Hetty could see her apprehension melt away.

Stewie continued. "It's like Rembrandt or Picasso or somebody famous like that did it, only it's better, because Troy didn't give my mom two heads or stupid looking eyes—but I'm not saying he couldn't if he wanted to. Wait till you see it!"

Hetty mouthed a question to Sophie. "The portrait? He finished?"

She nodded.

Stewie's voice squeaked, and he stood a little taller to make up for it. "Oh! and it's a shower, too. You know, a party where they play games and give people stuff. So, you could all bring a present if you want, but everybody knows it's not a *shower* kind of shower. Like with water."

Sophie's face was quite pink. For someone who was dreaming this up as he went along, Stewie certainly was holding their attention.

Troy whispered to him, and he brightened. "Here's what they want . . ." He turned back to Troy, and they whispered back and forth again. "Okay, so here's what you're supposed to bring—*advice*. That's what they really, really want."

Following the pattern previously set, Stewie raised his glass and said, "Bombs away!" The others did the same.

Hetty glanced at Kenzo and Mr. Kawada. Swept away in the general excitement, they seemed perfectly happy.

The evening was officially declared a success. Hetty caught Sophie's eye and learned it would be fine to take desserts up to Troy's room.

The one casualty of the evening was Miko.

CHAPTER TWELVE

Opportunity

Hetty and Miko walked up the stairs to Troy's room, while the others took the elevator.

Hetty could tell Miko needed to talk, so she lingered on the landing. "Did your father surprise you about Kenzo?"

"Yes." Miko's voice was shaky. "What am I going to do? Father has piled on another obligation. I'm sure he means well. It was supposed to make marriage to Kenzo more appealing, but I just feel trapped." Hetty gave a tissue to Miko, who wiped her tears. She sniffed, then followed Hetty up the stairs to face Kenzo and her father.

Stewie greeted them at Troy's door, and as they entered, they saw the large portrait of Sophie. Hetty thought it was far more beautiful than Stewie had said. She noticed the signature and pointed it out to Morgan. It was signed with the name *Sofé*, like on his mother's portrait.

Morgan snapped his fingers. "So! That's why we didn't make the connection."

Troy nodded. "It's because the French pronounce Sofer that way."

Hetty said she thought the painting captured Sophie's grace and amiable expression beautifully. "I can tell the artist cares a great deal about his subject," she said. Sophie put her hand in Troy's.

Katrinka had not been the center of attention for a while, so she sweetly claimed the spotlight. "I would *never* want a portrait painted of myself," she said. "Fashion changes so *dreadfully* fast. Sophie honey, I hope your hairstyle won't look out of date too soon."

Gracefully, Katrinka turned her attention to Miko, then smiled and fanned her eyelashes. "Miko, darling, I'm absolutely *delighted* for you! I've never heard about getting rich that way, but you're going to look real pretty in a kimono!"

Suddenly Hetty felt exhausted. She wondered why. Was it from walking up the stairs? The stuffy room made her queasy, and she backed up to approach the door.

Morgan supported her with an arm around her waist. "You look pale," he said. "Are you all right?"

When they opened the door to get some air from the hall, they were surprised to see a slim young man standing there. He appeared Japanese. Hetty asked if he might be looking for someone.

"Yes, I'm John Ito—a friend from the states—looking for Miko Kawada." His handshake was firm, and his voice deep and friendly.

He had to be Miko's boyfriend. Hetty wondered if he and Miko would rather see each other alone. She was about to suggest the idea, when he saw Miko. He winked at her and smiled broadly. Even though John said he didn't want to interrupt the party, Troy insisted that he enter.

Miko looked at Hetty nervously and moved behind her as if to hide. Maybe she dreaded introducing John to Kenzo. Was she hoping for some miraculous occurrence to delay it? When there was no avoiding the introduction, she said quietly, "John, meet my . . . my brother Kenzo."

In a breathless whisper, Miko asked Hetty to meet with her privately. They went in the bathroom, where rags, tubes of paint, and a jar of turpentine littered the counter.

Before Miko closed the door, her tears began to flow. "John shouldn't have surprised me like this. Why did he do it?"

"Well, if he had asked, would you have told him not to come?"

"Of course."

"Then that's why."

"Oh, Hetty! Isn't he wonderful? When he's around, how am I supposed to think?"

"I don't know. I never could."

Miko was surprised. "Really? That's exactly what Father was worried about," she said. "I need to be sensible."

"Yes. Sensible." Hetty nodded. "I think that's the best idea." The smell of turpentine was making her light headed."

"So, you agree? You think he should go home, too." Miko looked disappointed with the verdict.

"I didn't say that." Hetty felt nauseated. She found the turpentine lid and screwed it on.

Miko blew her nose on a square of toilet tissue. It disintegrated as if demonstrating how messy relationships could be. She washed her hands. "Then what *are* you saying?"

Hetty remembered feeling insanely irrational about Morgan, and she was grateful to the people whose judgment she valued. "I'm saying if it's possible, why not have it *both* ways? When your father gets to know John, he'll be able to advise you better. The most sensible match might actually be John. Your father may feel that way too."

Miko stared in the mirror for some time, as if her image might hold the answer, and a sudden smile indicated it did.

"Till now I couldn't make a decision," she said, "but tonight my father chose *for* me."

"Why do you say that?" Hetty asked.

"Because I'm an American girl." Miko laughed. "And American girls don't marry their brothers!" She was suddenly serious. "I wonder if I'll always be cursed with straddling two cultures."

With the turpentine fumes contained, Hetty felt a little better. "Cursed you say? I think it's more like an opportunity."

The Real Reason

Hetty and Morgan hurried to the park to find John. They found him waiting at the prearranged spot—a cluster of rocks where they could sit facing one another. While Miko was back at the hotel with her father and Kenzo, they could meet only briefly.

After a short greeting, John began. "Miko told me about the two of you. I know Hetty rescued Miko's father, and I think you understand what that means in the Japanese tradition."

Morgan nodded. "We have some idea."

John continued. "It means you have a unique relationship with Kawada-san. And quite frankly, I hope to benefit from it."

Morgan indicated they had expected as much.

John continued. "Miko's an extraordinary girl. My parents were not happy with me for letting her get away. We seemed so right for each other that I just took it for granted everything would fall naturally into place. I don't want to make that mistake again."

His pause was an expression of regret. "My father was her professor," he said, "and she was his favorite student. In fact, he's the one who introduced us. Don't you think Miko's father would respect that?"

When Hetty and Morgan both agreed, John began again.

"I don't think Kawada-san knows how bright she is and what a sacrifice it would be for her to stop her education. She says she can't marry Kenzo now that he's her brother. But I'll tell you the real reason. Her schooling is too important to her. Miko will want to reach her potential, and she'll need a man who believes in her. I want to be that man."

John laughed. "I hope to make Kenzo my brother-in-law."

Garlic Butter

As they waited for their flight to begin, Morgan fastened his seatbelt. He checked to see if Hetty seemed all right but said nothing about it. Though she had looked pale at the party yesterday, he knew Hetty never wanted attention to focus on her heart condition.

Before leaving the hotel, they had held a final conversation with their friends and exchanged addresses with them. Sophie and Troy promised to send wedding pictures.

Katrinka insisted that at the earliest possible opportunity she would need to teach Hetty a few beauty tricks. Otherwise, how on earth could she expect to hold onto her husband!

Based on Morgan's recommendation, Mr. Kawada would send Miko back to Stanford. If John wanted to marry her, he would have to prove himself. There was no hurry now, and he liked John. Besides, as heir to Mr. Kawada's business, Kenzo seemed content with being his son by agreement.

Morgan locked his seat upright. Overjoyed to be on the way home at last, he hoped Hetty felt the same. In a recurring dream, he felt a frantic need to know she was his in every way. So eager was he to solve their marriage issues, that he could think of little else. He asked, "Are you disappointed to go home without seeing Tokyo?"

He hoped she would proclaim a desire to be with him alone—to share the same pillow and laugh together in the middle of the night.

"Not really," she said. "I know Mr. Kawada's invitation still stands. But it's a shame we'll be missing Stewie's birthday party."

Morgan watched the beat of her pulse in the soft curve of her neck. Whenever his beard might be too rough against her face, he liked to kiss her there.

"Yes," he said. "Stewie was ready to announce a combined wedding and birthday party with an octopus theme."

Hetty laughed and blinked. Her pale lashes captured the light from the window. "I heard," she said. "I told him it would be a special delicacy if the wedding was a separate event and they serve it to the guests."

Morgan smiled. "So, that's why he asked how octopus tastes!"

Hetty's cheeks were soft and pink. He wanted to sit under the rose trellis at the cottage and hold her tight.

"What did you tell him?" she asked.

Her lips were moist and sweet and he wanted to kiss them. "Tell who?" he asked.

"Stewie."

"Oh, I told him they taste like rubber bands."

Hetty laughed. Her eyes were blue as the sky and they were watching him as if she never wanted to look away.

"Don't you think it's like the emperor's new clothes?" she asked. "I mean, maybe everyone thinks octopus tastes like rubber bands, but nobody wants to admit it."

Hetty's hand touched his, quite by accident. "And the same about snails." She blushed but didn't move her hand. "What do *they* taste like?"

"Snails taste like snails," he said. "That's why they have to call them escargots and sauté them in garlic butter."

He didn't want to move his hand. He did anyway, because their unspoken understanding required it.

He stated the obvious. "Not all things are what they seem."

She dipped her head. "But you are," she said.

"You mean I'm the same with or without garlic butter?"

The Cottage

Morgan whispered, "We're home." Hetty awoke to find her head on his shoulder. Too exhausted to support herself, she had fallen asleep during the taxi ride.

Her eyes opened to see their small stone cottage. Enclosed by a white picket fence, it was a sight she remembered in sweet detail. As Morgan helped her from the taxi, she felt the familiar aura of kindness about the home and its surroundings. It promised a reverence for kindly thoughts and gentle love.

While Morgan paid the driver, Hetty breathed deeply. A warm afternoon breeze carried the sweet, earthy scent of boxwood. Dappled light danced through the lacy foliage of the adjacent forest.

Skirting the fence was a garden of zinnias and tall pink hollyhocks, while on both sides of the gate, pink and yellow roses climbed the trellis. The gate was slightly ajar, as if awaiting their arrival. It opened onto a path of carefully laid stones with baby tears and soft green mosses in the chinks. Watchful not to disturb the velvety softness, they crossed the stepping-stones to the front porch.

The ivy arching over the front door required a little trimming, though not enough to disturb the family of sparrows nesting in it.

Several large rocks served as the front steps to the cottage. Morgan suggested that Hetty sit there while he carried the luggage inside. From there she could watch the bluebird house her father had secured to the picket fence. The violets at her feet had become unruly, and the lavender phlox was spreading with charming abandon. Yet the garden appeared well loved in spite of their neglect.

For as long as she could remember, the wrought-iron latch had needed oiling. It squeaked now as Morgan opened the front door. He carried the suitcases up the stairs, then she heard nothing for a time. Maybe he was unpacking.

Hetty listened to the stillness and imagined planting herbs and flowers. Surely by tomorrow she would regain the necessary energy to begin. They might even want a small cherry tree they could watch growing over the years. Tilting her head, she felt the sun on her face. It gave a pleasant warmth to the rest of her thin frame as well.

She closed her eyes, relishing the small and quiet things she remembered so well: the trees whispering in the breeze; the birds calling from the woods; and the smell of the rich, fertile soil.

Hetty felt a tiny, almost imperceptible flutter. In recent years, she had been eager to know about the beginnings of life—to learn how that miraculous quickening might feel. She felt it now. Once more it came—like butterfly wings, or a kiss from an angel. She was sure of it. Whatever the reason for the sudden awareness, she was not mistaken.

How should she think about something so completely unexpected? Instinctively she knew there would now be new purpose to her life. She would smother her disappointment about law school. The deadline to decide was supposed to be tomorrow.

The joy she felt far outweighed her fears, and she smiled.

I can hardly believe this miracle—the honor of bearing Morgan's child! We vowed not to keep secrets, but how can I tell him now? He'd be frightened if he knew. Maybe after I've seen the doctor . . .

Morgan came down the stairs and exclaimed about the pile of mail Swenson had collected for them during their absence.

Soon Hetty heard a low chuckle. Then amusement became an explosion of unbridled mirth. Turning toward Morgan, she saw his head thrown back in exultant, full-blown laughter. Clutching a paper, he stumbled to the porch and sat next to her on the step. In her hands, he placed the reason for his good cheer.

On a small note Swenson had scrawled the words, *I found this in today's paper.* It was fastened to an article he had circled with a dark pen. Together they read it.

Retraction and Apology:
In the Tilly Tells All column of July 28, Tilly Teller stated incorrectly that the marriage between Morgan Morganthal and Henrietta Lawrence is presumed invalid.

Tilly regrets quoting a source that has since proven unreliable and hereby retracts the statement with her deepest apologies.

Better Than We Knew

Morgan was free to put his arm around Hetty's waist, so he did. Sitting on the step with her, he was completely absorbed in her nearness. Her eyes were the color of the sky on a perfect day, and her hair spilled lightly over her shoulders in undisciplined puffs. His eyes wandered from the dimple in her chin to the pale lashes that rimmed her eyes.

The small suggestion of a secret smile enthralled him, and Morgan's throat tightened with his rapid breathing.

"Morgan . . ." she said, "we had the perfect honeymoon, and now it's even better than we knew." Her lips parted as if to say more.

"Yes," he said, "and I won't have to visit the county clerk. It wasn't all sunshine and roses. But maybe that's not the point of a honeymoon."

She blinked and said, "I know you're right. Maybe it was a way to learn about each other. I wouldn't have changed a thing." She laughed. "I even got to see you some of the time."

Her lips were the soft pink of the roses on the trellis. He wanted to hold her . . . to cradle her and keep her safe.

Morgan had been waiting for the right moment. When it came, he stood. "Now for the threshold," he said. She was light as gossamer. He lifted her, and she rested her head in his neck. He carried her past the stone fireplace, around the piano, and up to the loft. Morgan knew her favorite spot, and he took her where the sun was brightest in the afternoon.

He smiled broadly. "See anything new?" Below the windowsill was her papa's desk. She had admired it since she was a child. Morgan explained, "I called Dan, and he brought it here yesterday."

She was delighted to see it, and said, "Oh, Morgan! You're going to love using this desk. I can't wait to show you all the secret compartments!"

Hetty didn't seem to understand it was for her, and she didn't notice his present sitting in the middle of it. He had wrapped it quickly while Hetty was waiting on the front porch. Now he was embarrassed it was such a lumpy, sorry-looking thing. His cheeks colored, and he cleared his throat. Pulling it toward her, he said, "I'm not great at wrapping things."

Just inside was his message. Morgan had waited to put it there at the last minute, in case he should decide to change his mind. The note read, *For Hetty, my future law partner. Love, Morgan.*

It was the desk set from Paris.

Hetty's eyes were large and moist, and they shone with eager devotion. Was she laughing or crying? Morgan could only guess at the range of her emotions as she smothered him with kisses. She was such a delightful mystery! Morgan wondered at her breathless radiance and smoothed back her hair.

He knew the sweet tenderness of her love. It came from a full heart, bursting with grateful affection. She was his in every way.

THE END

Hetty knows the secret to lasting love. But Katrinka, Morgan's beautiful former fiancée, schemes to destroy their happiness. Can Hetty prevail with her selfless love and trust?

Find the answer in the fifth book of the Hetty series: *Hetty on Hold*.

Honeymoon Summer is the fourth novel in the Hetty series by Martha Sears West. It follows *Hetty, Hetty Happens,* and *Hetty or Not.* It is followed by *Hetty on Hold.* Her book titled *Rhymes and Doodles from a Wind-up Toy* is a collection intended for all ages. She has also written and illustrated two children's books: *Longer than Forevermore,* and *Jake, Dad and the Worm.* All Martha's books have received the Mom's Choice© Award for excellence in family-friendly content.

COLOPHON

The Bembo Typeface

Bembo is a classic typeface that displays the characteristics that identify Old Style, humanist designs. It was drawn by Aldus Manutius and first used in 1496 for a 60-page text about a journey to Mount Aetna by a young humanist poet, Pietro Bembo, later a cardinal and secretary to Pope Leo X.

More recently, Bembo is the typeface used for volumes in the Everyman's Library series. Monotype Bembo is generally regarded as one of the most handsome revivals of Manutius' 15th century roman type.

The font size of the italic sections in *Honeymoon Summer* is 12.5; otherwise, font size 12 has been used in the body of the text.